Bullshit History

Bullshit History

Stories from history you've never
heard of…
because they're completely made up

Nick Hall

Published by Vulpine Press in the United Kingdom in 2024

ISBN: 978-1-83919-559-4

www.vulpine-press.com

Contents

Introduction

Ever heard about the only African Pope in history, the horse that swam the English Channel, or the town that hung a baguette?

No?

That's because I just made them up.

FAKE is everywhere. Our newspapers spout it, our politicians exclaim it, and our celebrities thrive on it. It seems like nowadays you can make up any old tosh and people will just swallow it without one iota of common sense.

So why should history miss out on all the fun?

Here are tons of characters from history for you to amaze your friends and family with – safe in the knowledge that they're all complete and utter bullshit.

Royalty and Rulers

The Spanish King Who Banned Shitting

King Carlos was a minor figure in the history of Spanish royalty. The son of King Louis of Castille, he never won a battle or brought riches to his subjects, but he did have a major influence on their toilet habits. This is because the blue (or brown) blooded Carlos had a life-long aversion to taking a dump. His fear of faeces can be traced back to an unfortunate incident in childhood when the sickly prince fell through the wooden hole in his private latrine and became trapped in the foul-smelling chamber below. Fished out several hours later by his courtiers, Carlos was traumatised, and the number one in line for the throne harboured a psychological aversion to number twos for the rest of his life.

Years later, a more Freudian rumour alleged that his mother, Queen Phillipa, unable to take her eyes off her only son for just one second, would drag him into the toilet whenever she needed to go. From here, she would complain endlessly about Carlos' father while using the facilities.

After taking the throne in 1451, he demanded that no one in his court, nobleman, courtesan or servant, was allowed to drop a log, as 'this revolting and unnatural act is a defiling of the pure body of Christ and indicates the growing of a tail – the serpent of the devil'. This extreme royal proclamation was initially considered an idle threat until a young nobleman was found using the privy a few days later. The furious king had him thrown from the castle turrets as punishment. From then on, the latrines were boarded over, the chamber pots smashed to smithereens, and no one in the castle ever went for a poo.

Except, of course, that wasn't true; it's just that everyone started doing their business in secret. Most people crept out in the middle of the night to squat behind the castle walls, while the wealthy could pay for their deposits to be squirrelled away in secret. A sewage black market quickly emerged, and prices for doodie disposal skyrocketed. The waste items were disguised as presents for distant family members or hidden in casks of wine.

Eventually, summer arrived and the smell from the open sewer outside the castle got so bad that the king twigged what was happening. Carlos was livid. He'd been betrayed, and the nauseating odour was inescapable. Since the culprits included every single bottom owner, the king couldn't punish them all. Instead, he sulked in his royal chambers while suffering from acute constipation. A rumour circulated that he could only visit the loo whilst absolutely hammered so that he would have no memory of it the following day.

In an ironic twist of history, King Carlos caught dysentery six months after taking power and died. The feeble king spent the last few weeks of his life living out his worst nightmare – being unable to stop shitting. When he eventually passed away, his citizens rejoiced by waving toilet paper out of their windows before rushing to re-open their latrines and go about their natural business. The 'waving of the toilet paper' is an annual tradition still carried out by some Castilian towns to this day.

The Only African Pope in History

There's been quite a lot of shitty popes throughout history. A rogues'gallery of ne'er-do-wells and psychopaths that have sat on the papal throne over the years. But what all these popes have in common is one thing, a lot of melanin. That's right; every single pope has been white. All except one.

Emperor Muboto was one of the wealthiest rulers the world has ever seen. He came to power in the Thirteenth century, and his empire covered much of modern-day Sudan and Chad. This valuable kingdom was littered with gold mines, and pretty soon, Muboto had more gold than he knew what to do with. His imperial palace was covered in gold, his outfits were embroidered with it, and bars of gold were even used to wedge the doors open.

But Muboto was bored. By age thirty, he had subjugated all the rival warlords in the region, and now he wanted to see the world. So, in 1231, he and his royal courtiers set off on one of the largest gap years ever. His journey would take seven years and was quite a sight to behold. The baggage line of camels and caravans was said to stretch for ten miles, bringing a vast array of cooks, soldiers, concubines, advisors, and thirty tonnes of gold.

His travels took him through North Africa, where they first stopped in Egypt. The emperor marvelled at the Great Sphinx, although one of his men took umbrage at the sight and tried to slice off his nose. The group then sailed across the Mediterranean and eventually reached the great city of Rome. Its citizens were astounded to witness a giant array of tents appear outside their walls one day, an ostentatious display of very aggressive glamping. Concerned that their new dark-skinned neighbours had come to invade, they readied themselves for war.

After entering the city gates to thousands of curious onlookers, the papacy invited Muboto and his entourage on a personal tour of the Vatican. The emperor was suitably impressed by the spectacle and, at the end of the tour, innocently asked if he could sit on the papal throne. After stifling their laughter, the cardinals explained that such an honour was reserved for God's anointed representative on earth, to which Muboto explained that he would happily pay for the privilege. Then he presented one hundred chests of gold at their feet.

After years of infighting, the papacy was virtually bankrupt, and they greedily accepted the offer. Muboto became pope for a week while the real pope disappeared to his summer residence on the coast. While on holiday with Muboto's cash, the emperor swanned around the Vatican wearing the papal crown as camels grazed in the gardens.

The new pope instigated a few changes that proved quite popular. For the first time in history, he opened the palace doors to visitors so ordinary Christians could see the opulent lifestyle of their spiritual leaders. Instead of being given a wafer at mass, worshippers were presented with a gold coin, which saw church attendance rates rocket. Muboto gave the church a go but ended up getting drunk on communion wine and falling asleep. One bishop tried to convert the new Pope to Christianity but was politely rebuffed. Muboto saw himself as a self-appointed god on earth, so he didn't have much spare time for the scriptures.

After the week was up, the cardinals inquired whether Muboto would like to buy another week as pope. However, by then, the emperor had grown bored of Rome and wanted new sights to behold. So, the caravans rolled on, and the previous pope returned sheepishly to an angry capital that wanted answers about the corruption. He discovered that Muboto had pinched several valuable paintings and a rare copy of the bible as souvenirs and liberally sprinkled the city with several tons of camel dung.

The emperor and his entourage headed north through Italy but turned back when they encountered the freezing snow of the Alps. They travelled southeast across the Mediterranean and eventually reached the Middle East, where Muboto spent several more years exploring the Muslim world. He must have found it more appealing than Christianity, as the African leader converted to Islam before returning home.

The Quarrelsome Duke Who Fought 97 Duels

Vladimir Wisnosky, a seventeenth century duke from the Grand Duchy of Lithuania, was one of the most argumentative men to ever have lived. The duke had a hair-trigger temper and would pick an argument with anyone he encountered. His nursemaid even claimed he started a row with her on the day he was born after finding fault with the temperature of her breast milk.

If there was one thing Vladimir loved more than arguing, it was fighting. His father, Duke Olaf Wisnosky, had him fencing from the age of five and young Vlad first accompanied his papa into battle at the age of twelve. Personal honour was considered a big deal in the Wisnosky family, and Duke Vladimir was raised to take offence at the slightest insult and to settle the matter with a duel. This made schooling particularly difficult, and the teenage duke was taught to challenge his private tutors whenever he received bad grades. One teacher's snarky comment about his poor grasp of Latin earned him a nasty cut to the shoulder.

Duke Vladimir fought 97 duels over his lifetime, averaging one every six months. He fought his first duel at the age of ten after he lost out to a rival schoolmate over a girl's affections, and by the time he was twenty, he had duelled most of the minor royalty in Lithuania. Over the years, he went on to duel with his best friend, godson, gardener, hairdresser, milkman, priest (twice), servants, and two of his ex-lovers, one male and one female.

You would think this amount of duelling led to a lot of death, but Vladimir usually stopped the fight once his opponent yielded, then picked them off the ground with a hearty laugh and gave them a big bear hug. Nowadays, he might be diagnosed as being manic depressive.

Often, when feeling despondent, the duke would head to the local pub and seek out a stranger or two to find insult with. Once he had duelled a few rounds with them, he would declare himself satisfied and buy everyone drinks for the evening. Of course, he didn't get away without suffering several injuries himself over the years. These included a punctured lung, two stunted fingers, three broken ribs, a pierced buttock, and a missing earlobe.

Duke Vladimir became so famous throughout Europe for quarrelling that no one in court would meet his eye for fear of falling foul of his temper. He was said to have challenged a nearby river to a duel after it flooded his lands and ruined his crops. He spent an hour stabbing at the water until he caught a cold and had to retreat to his bed, after which he considered the matter dealt with.

As the duke got older, Lithuania came under attack from neighbouring Russia, and the stresses started piling up. Vladimir sought solace in drink, which only made his temper worse. He had a blazing row with his brother over their inheritance and challenged him to a duel. The brother demurred, but Vladimir was insistent and killed his sibling in a fit of rage.

Struck dumb with horror, the duke fell to his knees in remorse. He claimed afterwards to have been visited by an angel, although witnesses insisted he was drunk and that it was a pigeon. No matter, Vladimir went straight to the local monastery, took the habit, and became a monk overnight. The monastic life didn't come easy to him at first. He challenged at least one monk to a duel after they cut in line at breakfast, but over time he learned to meditate, which helped his anger management enormously.

He spent his days reading books in the monastery and tending to his allotment. His years of sword fighting turned out to be useful when it came to trimming hedges and cutting back shrubs. But late at night, he could never quite rid himself of the memory of his former life and fondly recalled the excitement of his old ways. In the end, the records say he died of boredom while reading a book about seeds.

As a final note, Duke Vladimir's missing earlobe turned up in a local museum a century later, although doubters claimed that the shrivelled item belonged to a peasant. No matter its authenticity, the earlobe was said to have spiritual powers and became a religious relic. It was gifted to the monastery, and people would visit it to pray for an end to any long-running disputes they had. The ear was finally lost when the Nazis swept through Lithuania during the Second World War and destroyed the monastery. Lithuanians claim that Hitler, with his love of the occult, had the ear on a chain around his neck until his death.

The French Royal Who (Almost) Couldn't be Killed

During the 1780s and 90s, 'Madame Guillotine' struck fear into the heart of the French aristocracy, as revolutionary fervour sent hundreds of members of the nobility to their deaths in front of cheering crowds. And yet one royal managed to escape her deathly clutches quite a few times.

Jean-Phillipe LeToussier was a minor aristocrat owning a small amount of land in Burgundy and employed five servants. However, he was public enemy 'numero un' to the local revolutionaries. One day they stormed his meagre chateau and carted the unfortunate landowner off to prison. Jean-Phillipe was sentenced to death at a rigged trial, beginning a nerve-shredding year for him.

After languishing in the cells for weeks, his execution date was finally reached, and the nobleman marched into the town square. In front of a large crowd, Jean-Phillipe was led up the stairs onto the makeshift stage, and his head placed in the guillotine. The executioner released the rope, but at the crucial moment the blade failed to fall. The deadly device had malfunctioned! The guillotine's creator, a local blacksmith, was summoned to the scene, but even he had trouble making it work. After several hours of waiting, the crowd became impatient, as a local boules match had been scheduled for the same afternoon. Ultimately, it was decided to take the relieved prisoner back to the cells and try again another day.

A revised date was agreed, and Jean-Phillipe was brought back out for his second execution. This time a fistfight started in the crowd over who had the best view, and it quickly spread throughout the townsfolk, fuelled by local grievances and hungry bellies. The revolutionaries abruptly abandoned the execution, and everyone involved fled back to the safety of the prison as rioting engulfed the town for a whole week.

A third attempt at executing Jean-Phillipe was attempted. However, the priest overseeing the event dropped dead of a heart attack. Thinking quickly on his knees, Jean-Phillipe pleaded that he could not meet his maker without being read his last rites, and the devout locals agreed with the aristocrat. So back to the cells he went. The authorities were determined to kill Jean-Phillipe for a fourth time, but this coincided with a solar eclipse, convincing the superstitious locals that God was still annoyed with what happened the last time. So, the execution was postponed again.

By now, it was autumn, and a torrential downpour on the day of the fifth attempt flooded the market square, making executions impossible. On the sixth attempt, Jean-Philippe found himself joined onstage by a new intake of recently condemned aristocrats. He was scheduled to be guillotined last, but when it came to his turn, the cart was too full of bodies. The coachman refused to take any more on account of repetitive strain injury. After unsuccessfully demanding more money for his services, the coachman turned fully French and went on strike, so LeToussier survived again.

On the seventh attempt, Jean-Phillipe had finally scraped enough money from visitors and well-wishers to bribe his captors into 'forgetting' him. He also had enough left to celebrate Christmas in his prison cell with a roasted duck and a bottle of wine. The eighth execution saw an arctic cold spell descend on Europe, leaving the guillotine frozen solid. The local blacksmith made a valiant attempt to defrost the blade using his wee, to no avail.

The ninth attempt had Jean-Phillipe again joined by a crew of fellow aristocrats. One panicky prisoner broke free from his shackles and ran down a side street. The locals eventually discovered him cowering in the confessional of the local church. By now, it was three in the morning, and the executions were abandoned. The tenth attempt coincided with a plague outbreak in the region, and the resourceful Jean-Phillipe managed to fake black plague spots using coal stolen from the fireplace. The horrified jailors left him well alone for several months.

The eleventh and penultimate attempt at guillotining Jean-Phillipe was scheduled to go ahead. Then a new revolution broke out, and the previous radicals were arrested as traitors to the cause. Suddenly no one cared about one smelly old landowner. The following day the revolutionary old guard took his place under the guillotine blade. A bemused Jean-Phillipe watched from his prison window as his former jailors went to their deaths sobbing and wailing.

By the twelfth attempt, a whole year had passed since he was first arrested, and the locals had developed a soft spot for the plucky aristocrat. The original revolutionaries had been deposed, and no one could quite remember why Jean-Phillipe had been locked up to begin with. After taking to the stage for a final time, the crowd started chanting that he be set free, and, hoping to curry favour with the masses, the new authorities agreed.

Jean-Phillipe returned to his chateau only to discover that the original revolutionaries had burnt it to the ground. Rather than keeping his head down, he quickly became a celebrity and spent the next ten years touring France in his theatrical show entitled 'The man who defeated death'. By now, the revolution had petered out, and European society was enthralled by the aristocrat who had avoided the guillotine so many times.

Despite surviving public execution, Jean-Phillipe's death still came in front of a crowd. And it involved a guillotine. While performing his show for the thousandth time, he tripped on the prop guillotine rope, fell from the stage, and broke his neck. The audience roared with laughter, thinking this was part of the act. Then someone in the front row let out a scream. Madame Guillotine had finally had her revenge.

* Author's note: Nowadays, a French actor 'dying' onstage is known as a 'Jean-Phillipe'.

The Prime Minister who was Batman

Charles Grey was a pretty unexciting British Prime Minister. Serving for four years from 1830, Grey's government had few notable achievements. However, he found notoriety as the result of his secret night-time activities.

In 1832 the bookish and reserved PM was invited to spend the evening accompanying the newly formed Metropolitan Police in their activities. Grey followed the bobbies as they arrested pickpockets, investigated burglaries, and raided a warehouse selling stolen goods. The prime minister managed to trip up one of the culprits as they fled from the warehouse, and he returned to Downing Street giddy and enthused by what he had taken part in. Compared to his dreary life as PM answering equally dreary questions in the House of Commons, battling criminals in the shadowy alleyways of London was much more exciting. And so, the Prime Minister insisted on going out with the police on more nightly raids. His blue-blooded wife,

Francesca, found the whole idea of her husband running around in the dark most unseemly.

The Prime Minister's cabinet grew concerned that he might be injured or even killed in his activities with the police and pressured him to stop. Grey finally agreed to their demands, or so they thought. Charles had been bitten by the crime-fighting bug and vowed to become a secret street vigilante.

The prime minister started going out alone at night, determined to apprehend the city's vilest crooks. Only his Private Secretary knew the full extent of what was happening. He advised against it during a heated game of billiards, but Grey threatened him with a sock full of balls. Charles was determined to chase his thrill. Having sat behind a desk for most of his life, the normally timid prime minister had found a hobby that got his heart racing. To avoid recognition, he wore a sackcloth over his head with eye holes cut out and took to frequenting the narrow streets around St Giles and Soho. He manhandled criminals wherever he could find them and tied them up for the police to discover the next morning. He quickly gained the nickname 'the hooded menace', partly because he would often mistake innocent passers-by for criminals.

No one else suspected what the Prime Minister was up to. Although he was out for whole nights at a time, Lady Francesca believed he was spending his time in the gambling clubs of Mayfair, something which was fairly standard for MPs. After one tussle with a hoodlum Grey was stabbed in the shoulder and had to appear in the House Commons with his arm in a sling, explaining that he tripped on a Downing Street rug. To continue the ruse, the PM had to throw out his wife's favourite Persian carpet and smash a priceless Persian vase that sat above the Downing Street fireplace.

After months of action and lucky escapes, the prime minister's exploits finally came to an end. The police arrested Grey during a scuffle with robbers, and the Private Secretary was forced to reveal everything to Lord Melbourne, the Home Secretary. His Lordship rushed down to the police station to cover things up. By now, the penny papers were starting to smell a story. It was rumoured that King George IV was fighting crime on the streets, and it was only a matter of time before journalists rumbled who the real crime fighter was. The Secretary of State begged the PM to give up his unusual nightlife, and with a heavy heart, Charles agreed. His government folded soon afterwards, and he retired from politics, spending his remaining years on his estate in the North of England.

The crime-fighting bug never entirely left him. Now and then, the criminals of Newcastle were threatened by a hooded figure who emerged from the shadows and then disappeared into the night. No one knew who this mysterious stranger was. Meanwhile, Grey would show his drinking guests a curious bruise or recent scar. When asked how he came by it, the former Prime minister simply replied with a cryptic smile.

The Dictator Who Loved Plastic Surgery

Gurban Suryev was the ruler of Turkmenistan in the 1960s and 70s and turned out to be quite barmy.

His father, Anatoli Suryev, had taken power with the help of the neighbouring Soviet Union, and the family ruled Turkmenistan with an iron fist for decades afterwards. As a young man, Gurban was sent to finishing schools in Switzerland, where he became acquainted with the finer things in life. When his father died in 1965, Gurban was summoned home to take his place and 'elected' leader of Turkmenistan by 98.7% of the (no-doubt) joyful population.

Gurban had several vices, including partying, gambling, and expensive cars. However, his biggest weakness was vanity; he believed himself to be mind-blowingly handsome.

After taking power, Gurban demanded that his image be seen everywhere so that all citizens could bask in his good looks. Gurban's face was plastered on billboards overlooking the main boulevards, school assembly halls and even cereal boxes from the state cereal company. He went so far as to write and direct a series of movies with himself as the star. It was mandatory for Turkmenis to watch his films at the cinema. Using his country's oil wealth, he paid for cameos from Hollywood actors like Steve McQueen and Paul Newman.

As the years rolled by, his megalomania spiralled out of control. It wasn't enough that his subjects looked up at him; they had to look exactly like him.

In 1972 Gurban published a new decree that every citizen in the country should have plastic surgery in his likeness. He ordered surgery clinics to be installed across the country, with surgeons given clear instructions on what to carry out – eyebrow lifts, face pulling, and brow tightening. The problem was that there weren't any plastic surgeons in Turkmenistan, so doctors and nurses were bribed to switch careers. Once this news got out, people with no medical knowledge, such as taxi drivers and street cleaners, started lying on their application forms to become plastic surgeons for fast cash.

Unsurprisingly, state-enforced plastic surgery wasn't as high on people's wish lists as clean drinking water or round-the-clock electricity. So, take-up was non-existent. Most people bribed local officials to avoid undergoing the procedure, while the surgeons claimed fake quotas to receive their bonuses. As an alternative, a black market emerged, importing latex masks from neighbouring Iran made in the dictator's likeness so that people could appear as if they had undergone the procedure.

Eventually, the President twigged that people weren't seeing this as a wonderful opportunity. When driving through a town in his Presidential Rolls-Royce, Gurban demanded they pull over and inspect the local citizens for his likeness. Those working in the presidential palace were the unluckiest, as Gurban oversaw their procedures personally. The dictator claimed it made him feel safer surrounded by dozens of identical lookalikes. However, the surgeries were so shoddy that any would-be assassin would have identified the great leader. It was said that Gurban made his wife undergo the procedure so he could know what it was like to make love to himself!

In the end, Gurban's vanity brought about his own downfall. Full of hubris, he demanded that the head of the military undergo surgery and shave off his prized moustache. The 70-year-old general politely refused. Gurban was insistent. For the sake of his facial hair, the general had no choice. He instigated a military coup which saw Gurban and his family thrown out of the country.

The Suryevs moved from country to country as pariahs until settling in Indonesia many years later. As his looks deserted him, Gurban himself became addicted to plastic surgery. Without the funds to pay for quality work, the results became worse and worse. In a last bid to reclaim his supposed former glory, Gurban underwent a complicated procedure to have his face transplanted with that of an 18-year-old boy, but the aged dictator died of a heart attack on the operating table.

* Authors' note: Suryev's downfall put a stigma on removing one's moustache, and to this day, Turkmeni barbers will refuse to shave a customer's top lip.

Wars and the Military

The Husband and Wife Who Fought at the Battle of Hastings

While couples and fighting tend to go hand in hand, a marriage rarely gets caught up in a full-blown war. That's exactly what happened in 1066.

A yeoman from Shropshire enlisted to fight in King Harold's army against the invading William the Conqueror at the Battle of Hastings. However, the yeoman really didn't want to go as he had only been married the previous week. Rather than be separated, the newly-weds hatched a plan to take a very unorthodox honeymoon.

The yeoman's wife went to great lengths to dress up like a regular soldier, cutting her hair, muddying her face, and strapping down her womanly shape underneath chainmail and armour. Dressed like her fellow soldiers and putting on a masculine baritone, she stowed away with her husband. She took on the fake name of Edmund, but owing to her small size, the other soldiers soon started calling her 'Little Ed'. The disguise worked, and she could share a tent with her husband at night, although neighbouring soldiers must have been puzzled by the noises coming from inside.

And the two didn't go their separate ways once the battle started. The wife decided that since she'd come all this way, she might as well get stuck in. Reports claim that despite her slender frame, she wielded a broadsword with deadly force and took out several of William's soldiers. Rumours circulated that a marital argument broke out during the fighting, and 'Little Ed' was seen storming off the battlefield in a huff.

Whether the married couple survived the Battle of Hastings isn't known; however, the two lovers were recorded for posterity in the Bayeux Tapestry. Two amorous figures can be seen in the background near the battle's end, holding hands and staring into each other's eyes as the conflict over England's future rages.

The Chinese General Who Invented the Yo-Yo

General Tun-Yu was a Chinese military commander during the Ming dynasty. China at the time was being torn apart by a bitter twenty-year civil war fought between Tun-Yu's Emperor Lin and the Emperor's sister, or more accurately, her husband Shao, who wanted to claim the throne for himself.

With both sides worn down by the bloody conflict, Lin's brother-in-law agreed to come to the peace table and discuss an accord. Except General Tun-Yu wasn't having any of it. His anger towards the disloyal Shao had grown fierce over the years, and he was determined to defeat them once and for all, even without his emperor's knowledge.

Realising that he would be in the same room as Shao for the peace talks, Tun-Yu saw a perfect opportunity to kill the rebel leader and break the opposition. The problem was that Emperor Lin had demanded no one bring weapons into the room as a peace gesture to his nervous brother-in-law.

General Tun-Yu, therefore, required something discreet that wouldn't arouse suspicion, and it needed to reach across the table to strike Shao with deadly force.

Following a brainstorming session which allegedly also gave rise to a primitive version of the slinky, he devised a circular wooden spool on a string that he could fling across the room in an instant. The general had the spool lined with razor blades to slice the victim's neck open. In the run-up to the talks, Tun-Yu practised endlessly with the novel device, working on hay bales to achieve the precise angle and power of attack. He even threw in a few trick moves like 'walk-the-dog' and 'rock-the-baby' until he knew he was ready.

On the fateful day, Shao waited impatiently for the emperor and Tun-Yu to arrive. Eventually, they made their entrance, and the general was immediately searched for weapons, revealing nothing but a harmless children's toy. The general explained that he had been given the present as a good luck charm by his young son, which seemed to satisfy suspicions. And so, the meeting got underway.

The emperor and his brother-in-law conversed in the corner while Tun-Yu waited to strike. It seemed that Shao would never step out from behind Emperor Lin. Finally, at the end of the meeting, both men agreed to sign a peace treaty. As Shao leant forward to sign the document, the general saw his opportunity. Before anyone could blink, Tun-Yu pulled the yo-yo from his pocket and flung it forward, striking Shao in the throat. The rebel leader collapsed across the table, blood pouring over the treaty. He died before the ink on his signature had time to dry, although the blood had made a mess of the whole thing anyway.

The killing happened so fast that the room erupted in confusion and commotion, allowing Tun-Yu to shepherd his emperor to safety. With the rebels leaderless, they quickly fell apart, and Emperor Lin's sister promptly returned home and begged for forgiveness, distraught at her husband's untimely death.

Although Tun-Yu had secured victory for his emperor, Lin was horrified at the underhand manner in which it had been won and demanded that the general be put to death for the dishonourable act. Although facing execution, Tun-Yu showed no remorse and was still delighted that he had managed to end the war. He died with a contented smile on his face as he was struck through by his own sword.

After Tun-Yu's death, his men started carrying versions of the yo-yo in honour of their general until one enterprising soldier started selling them as children's toys, minus the razor blades. The toys proved wildly popular throughout China, although the emperor's sister was upset by the constant reminder. Nowadays, children all around the world play with this delightful little toy, unaware of its gruesome origins.

The Battle That Was Decided by Paper, Scissors, Stone

Scandinavia sometimes gets an unfair reputation for being a bit boring. A bunch of sauna-loving social democrats enjoying cross-country skiing and morbid TV detective shows. Actually, Scandinavians can be just as quarrelsome and conniving as the rest of us.

Nordic neighbours Norway and Sweden have a particularly stormy relationship. Their disagreements came to a notable head in 1789 when the Swedish Crown Prince Karl Johan and his opposing number King Frederick of Norway, fell out. It all started at a summit of European leaders when Frederick took offence at Karl Johan's failure to shake his hand. Returning the perceived insult, he took Johann's seat at dinner, to which the Crown Prince responded by talking through King Frederick's speech. Over the weekend, things got increasingly worse, and the summit ended with both leaders almost coming to blows.

Returning home, their hatred of one another escalated, and they issued orders to amass their armies and prepare for battle. What followed were months of skirmishes up and down the Norway-Sweden border. Karl Johan and Frederick were determined to defeat each other in combat and brought more and more troops forward.

By now, it was winter in Scandinavia, and the conditions for both armies were horrible. Carts and cannons were frozen solid in the mud, horses died of hyperthermia, and malnourished soldiers huddled in their tents desperately trying to stay alive. It was said to be so cold that urine would freeze in mid-air, leaving curious wee sculptures littering the ground. The commanders of each army, the Norwegian Major Christianson, and the Swedish Duke Ljungberg, both sent letters to their respective leaders, imploring them to delay the battle until the spring. But the animosity between the two was so great that each demanded their forces take to the battlefield the following day.

Both commanders were compassionate military leaders who didn't want to waste their men's lives for such a pathetic feud, so they decided to meet secretly to discuss ways of deciding the battle without any needless deaths.

The first suggestion was that two soldiers fight it out on behalf of both armies. However, the men were so malnourished that they couldn't go for more than two minutes, and the contest was abandoned.

In the end, they settled on playing a game of paper, scissors, and stone to decide who would win. The game in Scandinavia was known as birchwood, knife, and flint. The commanders selected a soldier from each side to play a best-of-three match in no man's land. Sweden took an early lead with flint over knife before the next two rounds ended in stalemate, birchwood each. Norway then managed to bring the score level with Birch over Flint. The game had to be paused when a bear ambushed the crowd. Eventually, it was scared off, and the tussle continued. Two more nail-biting draws continued before Norway secured a shock 2-1 win with a last-minute switch from flint to knife to beat birch. A fantastic comeback performance by the plucky Norwegian soldier!

Honouring the agreement between the two commanders, Norway was declared the winner of the battle, and the two wrote to their royal heads informing them of the result. They agreed to keep their little game a secret and concocted an elaborate story about an eight-hour battle costing many hundreds of lives. Each army was sworn to secrecy and faced with having to fight again in those conditions, everyone agreed to keep their mouths shut.

King Frederick was ecstatic when he received the victorious news, while Crown Prince Karl Johann was crushed. Luckily the outcome bore one crucial, if unfortunate, result. Still in a deep depression weeks later, Johann committed suicide while out hunting. His nephew Ralph succeeded him, and he got on famously

with Frederick so much that they agreed to invade
Russia the following summer, as all good friends do.

The Spy Who Impersonated A Sultan

By the 1790s, the Ottoman Empire was a shadow of its former self, with Sultan Mahmott II in constant disagreement with his neighbours to the East and West. A particular sore point was contested territory on the border of the Persian Empire, near modern-day Armenia. The Persians were determined to seize the region from their Ottoman rivals without causing an all-out war. They devised a cunning plan, using their top spy stationed in the sultan's capital of Constantinople.

Following careful planning, the spy snuck into the private palace one night when his courtiers had gone to bed. Finding the sultan sleeping, he drugged the ruler with a powerful Persian sedative made from valerian root. He hid his unconscious body in the vast walk-in wardrobe under a pile of jewel-encrusted coats. Borrowing the sultan's pyjamas, he sat in bed and waited for his courtiers to arrive the following day.

The only stumbling block was that the Persian spy looked nothing like the real sultan, so he drew the bedroom shades, complaining of a dreadful headache. To seal the deal, he had a fake moustache, dropped his voice a few octaves and stuffed a golden pillow under his pyjamas, giving himself the sultan's belly. In the early-morning gloom, his courtiers couldn't tell he wasn't the genuine sultan.

The fake sultan ordered that his military grand vizier visit his chambers immediately, an unusual request, his servants thought, given that he never usually let his ministers enter his bedroom. When the vizier arrived, the 'Sultan' declared that a tactical masterstroke had been revealed to him in a dream; all troops should be removed from the disputed region immediately. The horrified vizier replied that such an order would see them lose the territory for good, to which the sultan grew angry: so much so that his fake moustache fell off. He demanded that the vizier immediately fall to his knees and swear loyalty to cover the slip. This gave him time to replace the disguise, although the spy accidentally put the moustache upside down. Threatening to have his advisor beheaded if he didn't carry out the order, the terrified man fled the room to fulfil his sultan's request. A letter was sent by the fastest rider demanding that the garrison pull back from the region or suffer the cruellest death imaginable.

After the vizier had departed, the drugged sultan was pulled out from underneath the pile of coats and returned to his bed. The spy jumped from the royal balcony onto a nearby rooftop, using pillows from the bed to cushion his fall. From there, he slid down an adjoining minaret into the streets below and escaped from the palace undetected. He gave the golden pillows to a shocked beggar at the palace gates, who remarked that they were a gift worthy of a sultan.

The real sultan woke that evening with severe migraine and no recollection of what had happened that day. When he discovered that orders had been given to remove troops from the border, he was incandescent with rage and sent for his vizier immediately. Asked why he had carried out such an action, the visibly confused vizier claimed that he had carried out the sultan's order from that morning. The sultan had the unfortunate adviser thrown in jail while hurriedly sending another rider to reverse the order. Unfortunately, it arrived far too late and with the army gone, the Persians moved in and secured the disputed territory from further Ottoman attack.

Despite tearful protests that he had only been carrying out his ruler's wishes, the sultan had his military vizier beheaded. Since the sultan was prone to violent mood swings, the rest of the court was only too willing to believe that he had given the order. Sultan Mahmott II eventually doubted himself and went mad, not knowing the truth.

Meanwhile, the spy returned home triumphantly to Persia. Expecting fame and fortune, he was informed that his exploits could never be told for fear of starting a full-blown war with the Ottomans. As a reward for his silence, the spy was given a villa and a lifetime pension. The spy kept up his end of the deal until his deathbed, where he revealed the full story of the deception. To prove his claim, he was able to show off a pair of the sultan's slippers that he had stolen from the Ottoman bedroom all those years ago.

The British Town That Hung a Baguette

The British have a proud tradition of hating the French: 1066, the Battle of Agincourt, and the European Union. Disliking the French hit new heights during the Napoleonic Wars at the start of the nineteenth century. During this period, anything that looked or sounded vaguely Francais was regarded with deep suspicion. The modest seaside town of Salcombe in Devon escalated this peculiar national quirk to audacious new levels.

Roger Bucklehurst desperately wanted to launch a career in politics. For the previous ten years, he had unsuccessfully stood as the Conservative candidate for Parliament. This 'John Bull' character was a failed local hotelier, and his Whig rival seemed guaranteed to win the upcoming election. With the ongoing Napoleonic Wars, Roger saw his opportunity to achieve victory by taking advantage of good old-fashioned British xenophobia.

The wannabe MP recognised the anti-French sentiments of his local constituents and decided to play up to them. He began to warn loudly of a secret French plot to invade England by way of Salcombe and massacre the inhabitants. When several male townsfolk contracted syphilis, Bucklehurst claimed that the French had sent over the disease to weaken the men ahead of the invasion. When Bucklehurst himself contracted the same STD, he insisted it was clear proof of its nefarious French origins. And people started to listen to his warnings.

One night following a violent storm in the English Channel, a French merchant ship and its cargo washed up on the Salcombe shore. Picking through the shipwreck, befuddled locals discovered cases of French cheese and wine. Sampling the food and beverage himself, Bucklehurst declared it to be foul, which was unsurprising considering it had been lost at sea for a week. Sensing an opportunity to twist the knife further, he publicly declared all French food equally vile. This won him a smattering of local support. His gastronomic smear campaign started when he stumbled across a crate of French baguettes.

No one in Salcombe had ever seen a baguette before, and the townspeople were shocked by its weird shape. Bucklehurst seized the chance to whip up the electorate by parading the baguettes on a cart through the town. In his iconic booming voice, perfected during his teenage years spent working as the town crier, he described the offending bread as a 'foreign abomination', as well as 'a phallic symbol of the crudest form, a twisted and malformed essence of the Gallic nature when compared to the stout, sturdy and good-hearted British loaf'. At this point, he threw the soggy bread into the crowd, who quickly tore it apart.

And Bucklehurst wasn't finished there. The Sunday before the election, he had the last remaining baguette condemned at church by a local priest before putting the bread on trial for crimes against God and the English. Speaking to the packed gallery, he warned that baguettes were a sign of the oncoming onslaught, and the enraptured jury found the baguette guilty as charged. The spectacle concluded with the baguette hanging on the quayside before a cheering crowd. Bucklehurst had planned for the bread to hang there all week, but the seagulls had a different idea and quickly gobbled it up. It didn't matter, the baguettes had done their work, and the mood was febrile.

His Whig opponent appealed for calm, suggesting that a French invasion of Devon seemed unlikely. The mob drowned him out, and Bucklehurst was duly elected the new Member of Parliament for Salcombe.

Political success transformed his palette. Several years later, a newspaper exposé revealed that the notably anti-French Bucklehurst was seen eating in a French restaurant in Soho every Thursday, devouring plates of pâté, garlic and snails. He managed to survive the scandal by claiming he had no idea the restaurant was French and would avoid it from now on, even campaigning for it to be closed down. He served for the next forty years and became one of the most corrupt MPs in British electoral history, all thanks to a bit of bread and a lot of French hating.

Travellers and Explorers

The Viking Who Gave up
Pillaging and Founded Leicester

If you lived in Britain in the eighth and ninth centuries, nothing scared you more than the sight of Vikings rampaging over the horizon. Raiding parties from Scandinavia were a constant threat, arriving on British shores in their longboats without warning before moving inland to pillage, burn and destroy. They gained a fearsome reputation as hard-core fighters and even harder-core drinkers. Except they weren't all like that.

Gregor Sigmundssen was renowned as a sweet and gentle Viking. He liked going for long walks on his own, was a keen student of nature and even enjoyed writing Norse poetry. But similar to modern-day military service, Gregor was eventually forced to pick up his axe and join the Viking marauders sent to Britain in 920 AD.

The invaders sailed across the North Sea for a fortnight, while Gregor spent most of it below deck with sea sickness and missed out on all the drinking games. Once the Vikings reached England, they got stuck in straight away. To give Gregor his due, he gave pillaging a go but found he wasn't having any fun. The sight of blood made him feel queasy, and setting fire to every building they came across seemed such a waste. He was very interested in Anglo-Saxon architecture, but it was impossible to admire the roof thatching without someone setting it ablaze. He tried suggesting to his Viking comrades that they tone down the murder and mayhem. His appeals were met with roars of laughter.

After six months, Gregor decided he'd had enough. The final breaking point was being ordered to kill a cat, which was too much for the Scandinavian pacifist. Instead, he went AWOL, faking his drowning in a nearby lake and fleeing with the cat at night. He journeyed several hundred miles until he felt safe and came across a peaceful green spot by the river. Here he founded a commune on the site of what would become Leicester. The settlement was a place of peace and relaxation with clear rules for anyone who wanted to join – no fighting, no yelling, and a hard rule on no drinking.

As it turned out, other Vikings felt the same way. Whenever a new raiding party reached England, a few stragglers would scuttle off and seek sanctuary in Gregor's Viking retirement home. They harvested their crops, sang songs from their homeland, and even married a few of the locals. The location always remained a closely guarded secret.

Eventually, the Viking raiders started to get their arses handed to them by the Britons and stopped sailing over. However, the commune continued to thrive, a shining example of what happens when Vikings and Anglo-Saxons get on. Many hundreds of years later, the small village had grown into the town of Leicester, whose residents still possess a hefty amount of Viking DNA. If you go out in Leicester on a Saturday night, it's clear that Gregor's utopian mantra of 'no fighting, no yelling, and no drinking' has sadly gone to Valhalla.

The Explorers Who Forgot Their Flag

In 1903, Argentina and Chile wanted to be the first nation to reach the summit of Mount Churakunga in the Andes, located right on the border between the two countries. The race between nations was frantically close. Each team departed only days apart, and after two weeks of sledging and climbing, the Chileans had a slight upper hand. In the end, they beat the Argentinians to the summit by a matter of hours. However, there was a problem.

The Chileans had forgotten to bring their national flag in a rush to get there first. When the Argentinians arrived at the summit, they unfurled their flag and claimed the record. The Chileans were annoyed, and a fistfight broke out. The Chile team leader received a broken nose, and an Argentinian huskie got kicked down the slopes before order was restored. Both teams returned home bickering over who had won the race to Churakunga.

At the time, the official rules were clear. For a country to own the record, it had to mark it with its national flag. The Guinness Book of Records still records Argentina as having conquered the mountain first, despite continuing protests from the Chilean Government. Locals living at the foot of the peak on both sides still claim they hear huskies barking late at night, a spooky reminder that the resentment hasn't gone away.

The Industrialist Who Lived All His Life on a Train

Joseph K. Abrams was the Elon Musk of his day (without all that Twitter stuff). Born a penniless orphan in Kentucky sometime in the 1820s, he became a self-made millionaire by 25, making enormous profits in coal and steel. Abrams' true passion was for innovation and technology; in the 1850s, this meant the railways.

Railroad fever drove an industrial revolution in the US, and Abrams quickly jumped on board. He became a significant figure in the rail industry and travelled around the country to conduct his business in a state-of-the-art train. Abrams had always been slightly unusual, demonstrating what we would now diagnose as OCD. His habits included:

A fear of hats.

Never tying shoelaces on his right foot.

Refusing to eat any food at weekends that was coloured green.

Shortly after reaching his thirtieth birthday, Abrams started to develop acute agoraphobia, and his condition worsened. The industrialist took to living in his train more and more, until from the age of 32, he never left the comfort of the carriages.

Abrams managed to lead a full life for the next fifty years. The industrialist saw plenty of the United States despite being confined to a train. Everywhere he went, Abrams had new railway lines built ahead of him, allowing him to visit numerous locations, including the Rocky Mountains, the Mojave Desert, and even the beaches of California. He also managed to get married, although he was insistent that his new bride Catherine live on a separate train that followed right behind him. She could visit his carriage for one hour daily before returning to her quarters.

The tycoon had his carriage kitted out with the latest Victorian inventions, including a gramophone, sunroof, cinema, heating system and air conditioner. Thanks to Thomas Edison's involvement, he installed electricity, which operated electric windows and a power shower. At each destination, crowds flocked to see the curious business magnate and his famous train. Abrams was having none of it, drawing shutters across the windows as the train hurtled past.

His fear of leaving the train was tested at times. One night a fire broke out in the carriage, and Abrams refused to leave, even faced with the prospect of burning to death. Luckily, the train was passing Lake Erie, and the staff could put it out with buckets of water.

Another time, the train was caught up in a riot spilling into Chicago station, and Abrams had to barricade himself inside. A blizzard in Montana also trapped Abrams for two weeks, and he had to survive on a diet of canned tuna until locals arrived to help dig out the wheels.

Despite being confined to the train, Abrams continued to grow his business empire, and by the 1890s, he was worth over 30 billion dollars in today's money. With his vast wealth came enormous political power, and over the years, his train carriage hosted five different Presidents asking for his support. So influential a figure was Abrams that the funeral train of the deceased President Chester Arthur was halted so that Abram's carriage could take priority on the line.

Although Abrams had visited Mexico and Canada, his lasting wish was to see Europe, and at the age of eighty, his train travelled on a steamer ship across the Atlantic. The first place he visited was Britain. Arriving in Liverpool, a complicated system of pulleys hoisted his carriage onto the railway tracks, and away he went.

Coming from America, a land of boundless horizons and open spaces, the Victorian railway system in Britain was much more congested and crowded. Unfortunately, this would prove Abrams' undoing.

Annoyed by the endless delays and cancellations he came across, the train fanatic became increasingly irate. He suffered a massive heart attack while waiting six hours at a red signal outside Stevenage. Due to leaves on the line, his staff could not get him to the hospital in time, so the American industrialist passed away where he had collapsed – in Hertfordshire.

Abrams' body was kept on the train carriage and returned to the US the same way he had come, with some minor delays, of course. His will gave Catherine the lion's share of his wealth, a fitting reward considering she had followed him constantly for the last forty years, and the rest went to the maintenance of train station waiting rooms. A museum in Kansas offered to buy his train for a considerable sum. Instead, as per Abrams' instructions, the carriage was dismantled and melted down.

In keeping with his last wishes, his widow ensured his ashes were secretly buried underneath a train station somewhere in America. Five stations tried to claim the honour by renaming themselves after the iconic businessman; however, the true location has never been made public. So, if you're ever waiting impatiently for the next Amtrak to arrive, who knows, you could be standing right above Joseph K. Abrams.

The Knight Who Got Lost on His Way to The Holy Land

The Crusades were a glorious time if you were a European knight and you loved fighting. For nearly two hundred years, these medieval gentlemen-soldiers volunteered for a quest hundreds of miles across Europe and the Middle East. Driven by a religious proclamation to 'reclaim' the Holy Land, they travelled there in their thousands, returning home with stories of glory, battle, and blood.

Except for one knight who never managed to find his way there. So, he just lied about it.

Sir Thomas Crillick was a twelfth century English Knight who inherited Morchester Castle in Northamptonshire. He had a reputation for being headstrong, vain, and impetuous. The real problem was his appalling sense of direction. He reportedly got lost on his estate so many times that a servant would tie a bell to his horse, so they could successfully locate him if he disappeared. His sense of direction was so bad rivals jokingly claimed that Sir Thomas spent an extra six months inside his mother's belly, as he couldn't find his way out!

Crillick set off for the Holy Land in the summer of 1184. He had arranged to meet with a company of fellow knights at Dover and sail across the Channel with them. When he failed to rendezvous after several days, they set sail without him, figuring he would eventually catch up. In fact, the hapless knight had taken a wrong turn at Canterbury and headed west, ending up a hundred and fifty miles away in Wiltshire. A further course correction took the knight north until he found himself outside Wrexham.

Sir Thomas was too proud to ask for help and continued his bungled attempts to reach the Middle East. Six months had elapsed by now, and Sir Thomas was going around the West Midlands in circles. Rather than admit his mistake and suffer the embarrassment of returning home a failure, the proud knight kept up the ruse for another two years, choosing to take lodgings at an inn outside Worcester.

There he held court night after night, claiming to be a highly decorated Christian warrior now sworn to protect the common folk. Naturally, he was allowed to stay for free; he even married the innkeeper's daughter. Eventually, the rascally Crillick decided it was time to head home, and one day he fled, leaving behind his wife and a huge bar tab.

When he finally arrived back at Morchester Castle, everyone was delighted to see him. Sir Thomas quickly invented fanciful stories about his exploits in the Holy Land. People hailed him a gallant hero, with tapestries embroidered and songs sung about his deeds. He would have got away with it if he hadn't decided to write his autobiography. It was ghost-written by a local monk. Sir Thomas claimed unbelievable feats in battle, and the manuscript was circulated far and wide.

The book fell into the hands of fellow knights who had just returned from the Crusades. They were surprised to read about Sir Thomas' adventures, particularly his claims of fighting in wars that never took place and conquering cities that didn't exist. The boastful knight had let his imagination run wild, riding on elephants and battling crocodiles. Quickly rumbled, Sir Thomas became a laughing stock among the knighting fraternity. His wife finally tracked him down and demanded a substantial pay-off to cover the bar tab and other expenses.

Crillick retreated inside the walls of the Castle in embarrassment and was rarely seen again. Rumour has it he was so paranoid about getting lost that he moved down to the castle dungeons and lived out the rest of his days in damp squalor. Even several hundred years later in Northamptonshire, getting lost is known as 'Doing a Sir Thomas'.

The Only Humans to Fight on The Moon

Landing people on the Moon is among humankind's most incredible feats. The ambition, innovation, and bravery required to complete this journey are awe-inspiring. Teamwork among the astronauts is vital, as they must execute every little detail perfectly to avoid disaster. Unfortunately, humans are disagreeable and argumentative, particularly when confined to tiny spaces for over a week, as any caravan holiday will show. It was almost inevitable there would eventually be a punch-up in space.

The fight occurred during the Apollo 16 mission in 1972, the fifth Apollo expedition to successfully land on the Moon. As with all previous missions, the crew consisted of three astronauts: Commander John Young, Lunar Module Pilot Charles Duke, and Command Module Pilot Ken Mattingly. Young and Duke would land on the Moon as the most senior team members while Mattingly orbited in the command module twiddling his thumbs.

Like other missions, the three astronauts started their training years in advance, and Young and Duke did not get on from the start. When NASA picked Young as Mission Commander, Duke believed he had been passed over, so their relationship went downhill. Duke would turn up late for his commander's mission briefings, while Young constantly interrupted his number two to nitpick what he was saying. Things deteriorated over time. Duke got drunk on eggnog at the NASA Christmas Party and insulted the commander's wife, while Young refused Duke's request to bring a family photo on the mission, owing to a 'lack of space'.

The mission launched on the 16th of April and took four days to reach the moon. Being in such cramped and sweaty conditions ratcheted up the tension as the two men sniped back and forth all the way there. The arguing increased when Young discovered that against orders, Duke had stashed family photos in his bunk, along with a Kermit the Frog mascot. Young got his own back by playing his favourite country and western tunes over the intercom at top volume, which he knew Duke detested. Luckily the third astronaut Ken Mattingly was able to act as a peacekeeper amid the tension, but when the time came for the module to land, Young and Duke were on their own.

Duke was keen to set foot on the surface first, and Young insisted as mission leader that he would leave the capsule and plant the American flag. Both astronauts were supposed to spend the next few hours conducting scientific experiments on the surface. Young delegated most of the work to his junior and instead posed for photos, even finding time for a quick game of golf. Duke finally had enough. After being ordered to retrieve a nearby golf ball, he snapped and punched his superior. Owing to the bulky space suit, the hit didn't land too hard, but due to the weak gravity, it knocked Young clean off his space boots and back five feet. Furious with his subordinate, the mission commander clambered back to his feet and returned the favour. The two started scuffling in the moon dirt like intergalactic sumo wrestlers, knocking over the flag. At the sound of scuffles over the radio, Mission Control assumed something had gone wrong and prepared to abort the mission. Then they heard swearing followed by the word 'jerk-off'. Duke grabbed hold of the golf club and swung it at Young. The commander clambered back inside the spacecraft and locked Duke out. Playing the part of mediator, Mission Control intervened and told both men to take a ten-minute timeout.

Duke went for a walk, doing several laps of a nearby lunar crater, while Young practised his breathing. Reluctantly, the two men apologised, and Young unlocked the capsule door. They finished up and returned to the command module for the voyage home. It would take nearly a week to reach Earth, which allowed plenty of time for them to talk through their problems, refereed by Ken Mattingley.

After splashing down in the Pacific, Young and Duke became good friends and used their shared experience to teach future astronauts how to keep cool in heated situations. Publicly NASA hushed up the incident for fear of giving the Soviet Union a propaganda coup in the space race. On the official audio recording of the Apollo 16 mission, there is a curious twenty-minute gap while the astronauts are on the moon. NASA felt the American public wasn't ready to hear their space heroes call each other 'jerk-offs'.

The Gambler Who Swam the Atlantic

Edmund Murray was a wealthy businessman and alcohol magnate known for his oddities and love of a good wager. His finest moment came in 1913 when he made a bet with members of the London Piccadilly Club that he would become the first person to swim the Atlantic Ocean.

The members naturally considered the 3,000-mile challenge impossible and were confident they would easily take Murray's money. The bet was worth a staggering £5 million, or £500 million in today's money, and threatened to bankrupt the businessman if he lost. Murray had an ingenious solution.

The signed betting agreement stipulated that Murray must 'swim continuously from the port of Southampton to New York harbour without getting out of the water'. To comply with this requirement, Murray constructed a giant heated swimming pool on the deck of an ocean liner bound from Southampton to New York. Once the liner left England, he remained in the pool at all times, having his meals delivered to him and drinking brandy at night. Despite torrential rainstorms and sea sickness, Murray managed the three-week crossing in good spirits and only got out of the pool once the ship docked in New York.

He returned to England to claim his winnings, but members of the Piccadilly Club were furious at what they considered a dirty swindle. The row dominated high society and ended up in the high court where a judge ruled that, although Murray had 'behaved in a vile and underhand manner unbecoming of an Englishman', he had stayed within the written rules of the wager and could therefore collect his winnings.

Murray's victory saw him banned from the club. He didn't care. With his newly acquired millions, he set up a rival club on the opposite side of the street, which he made sure became the most prestigious and sought-after location in town. And taking pride of place in the centre of the club – was a swimming pool.

As a final addition to the story, Murray had originally planned to cross the Atlantic a month earlier; however, the liner was unwilling to have a pool built on the deck, so they sailed without him. The name of that ship was the Titanic.

Scientists and Inventors

The Farmer Who 'Invented' Gravity

Sir Isaac Newton is considered one of the most important and influential scientists of all time. In 1687 he published his theory of gravity, arguing that all bodies enact a force on each other depending on their size and distance apart. To help illustrate his discovery, Newton claimed that an apple hit him on the head while sitting underneath a tree one day, and suddenly the theory of gravity appeared to him. The bigger the entity (the Earth), the greater its gravitational pull on another object (the falling apple). The story was a popular hit, and by the time of Newton's death, his theory of gravity was an established scientific fact: so much so that a Cambridgeshire farmer tried to take credit for it.

By 1735 Thomas Clampton was down on his luck. With his farming business suffering yet another poor harvest, he was fast running out of money and hit upon a novel idea to make a quick buck. Realising that Isaac Newton had lived next door when he was alive, he sued the Newton estate, claiming that the apple tree that gave the scientist his gravity brainwave was on his land, so Clampton should receive a share of the profits from this work.

The only problem was that Newton had made the whole story up. His theory of gravity took two decades to complete, so the story about being hit on the head by a piece of fruit had been a marketing gimmick. Newton's estate threatened to counter-sue the fraudulent farmer, and Clampton quickly dropped his claim. But he wasn't finished yet.

Determined not to let the truth get in the way of a money-making enterprise, Clampton started to market his apple tree to the public as a site of great historical discovery. Within a few weeks, crowds were queuing to admire the famous tree for a hefty entrance fee.

Faux intellectuals from fashionable London salons arrived in their droves to have their portraits painted next to the tree and prove their Enlightenment credentials. You could even have an apple dropped on your head for an extra two shillings to see if this sparked any world-changing ideas. When this failed to deliver results, Clampton replaced it with an extra-large marrow to drop on people's skulls. This came to an abrupt halt when one visitor was knocked unconscious. The farmer even went as far as to pickle an ordinary apple in a jar, claiming this was the original fruit that had given rise to the renowned theory.

After a busy summer, the crowds started to dwindle, and one night a furious storm brought down most of the tree and, with it, Clampton's business. The enterprising farmer wasn't prepared to give up here and started a new business selling fake Thomas Gainsborough paintings. Eventually, the famous British painter got wind of the fraud and took Clampton to court, and he again ended up penniless.

The Chemist Who Lied His Way onto the Periodic Table

The periodic table is an iconic symbol of scientific discovery, displaying all chemical elements in a handy, concise, and informative fashion. Plus, it looks cool on a shower curtain. To discover and name a new chemical element and then have it occupy a square on the periodic table is one of the greatest successes a chemist can enjoy. It's often the result of years of hard work and sacrifice unless you're the Swiss chemist who, in 1922, lied his way onto it.

Born in 1880, Victor Hessler showed a passion for chemistry and went on to become a professor at the University of Zurich. The chemistry department at the university was world-renowned, and much of the faculty were prominent figures in the chemical science – apart from Victor.

His research was considered poor, his scientific mind limited, and his presentational skills unremarkable. A colleague notably commented he had all the hallmarks of an office clerk rather than a scientist. His most noteworthy experiment saw him investigate the quality of different binding agents in emulsion paint – quite literally as exciting as watching paint dry. The department would have sacked him years ago, but his wife Magda had an uncle who happened to be the university's vice provost. It was Magda that drove him to his life of fraud.

After suffering years of an unsatisfactory marriage, she finally snapped and announced she was bored of him and needed a divorce. She wanted to see the world, and her paint-staring husband wouldn't give her that. Hessler panicked. Faced with losing her and his position at the university, the Swiss chemist needed to make a grand romantic gesture and a diamond necklace wouldn't cut it. So, he decided he would name a new chemical element after her. Because he wasn't clever enough to discover one, he would have to make it up. After weeks alone in the laboratory, Victor Hessler proudly announced to the world that he had found a new chemical element named 'Magdanium'. His wife was delighted with the present and decided to take him back.

His colleagues expressed doubt that Hessler had made such an eminent find. However, as it brought renewed prestige to the faculty, his father-in-law was happy to bask in the triumph. To support his discovery of Magdanium, Hessler wrote a fake scientific paper and carried out a series of rigged experiments to prove its existence. The scientific community hailed his triumph, and soon, the chemist was invited to give sold-out lectures worldwide with his beaming wife in tow. Magdanium now took pride of place on the periodic table.

Hessler's career and love life seemed secure, but this new-found success would be his undoing. After being promoted to head of the department in Zurich, the big-headed Hessler began an affair with a young laboratory assistant. When she threatened to break off the romance, he tried to prove his devotion by repeating the same trick and soon announced the discovery of yet another chemical element, which he named Agathine.

Hessler's wife immediately became suspicious because she didn't know anyone called Agatha, nor did his fellow chemists. They decided to investigate Professor Hessler's unlikely success rate. Further examination revealed the fraud, and Hessler was quickly rumbled. Meanwhile, the gesture did nothing to appease the laboratory assistant, and she revealed the affair to his wife.

Both Magdanium and Agathine were scrubbed from the periodic table. Hessler was summarily dismissed from the university and divorced by his wife. He ended up working as a lowly office clerk for a paint company, which suited his demeanour no end.

Considering his efforts, he should have won the No-bel Prize for lying.

The First Victim of the Atomic Bomb

The world is grimly aware that the atomic bomb was first used during the Second World War on the Japanese cities of Hiroshima and Nagasaki. The blasts resulted in the deaths of over 150,000 people. The lesser known is the tragedy of the first person killed by a nuclear weapon.

On 16 July 1945, the Manhattan Project undertook its first and only full test of the A-bomb in the deserts of New Mexico, codenamed Trinity. The pressure to succeed in the war's last few weeks was immense, and every detail needed to be correct across the forty-mile test site.

One very junior scientist on the project was named Edwin Phillips. His job was to check sensors on the site that would take magnitude readings of the atomic blast. At the last minute, one of the devices malfunctioned, and Philip was forced to drive out into the desert to make repairs.

Unfortunately, his car broke down on the way back to headquarters, and Edwin found himself stranded in the middle of the test site. To make matters worse, he had forgotten his radio and could not alert anyone to his plight. In desperation, he left the car and started running frantically.

Assuming that everyone was outside the danger zone, a countdown was initiated. Edwin was seven miles from the bomb when it detonated, but this wasn't nearly enough to keep him safe.

Thirty seconds later, the unfortunate scientist was caught in the nuclear explosion as it swept across the desert. The American authorities only realised their mistake after finding the charred remains of his car. They covered up the accident for fear of the project being halted and proceeded with the bombing of Japan.

As a cover-up to his friends and family, a story was concocted that Edwin had gone swimming in a nearby lake the day before the test and presumably drowned. Years later, A darker rumour circulated that the Manhattan Project leaders had been notified of Edwin's absence during the bomb's countdown. They had made the gruesome decision to detonate anyway in a determined effort to finally win the war.

The Irish Monk Who Convinced a King to Drink His Own Wee

In 882 AD, Irish clansman Aed Finlith was crowned High King of Ireland, a prestigious title given to the most powerful warrior chieftain on the isle. King Finlith spent much of his time in battle and, within a few years, had defeated all other rivals to the throne. His position now seemed secure, but in his greed, King Finlith wanted more.

Christianity reached Ireland in the fifth century, and monasteries could be found across the island. With their books and learning, monks were considered the smartest people around, and one such monk, Clenned the Wise, was famed for his intellect. When not at prayer, the aged monk would spend his days studying what we would now call biology, chemistry, and astronomy. Some even claimed that he had discovered the secret to eternal life.

Upon hearing rumours of this discovery, King Finlith demanded that Clenned appear before him. After conquering his rival clan members, the king was determined to defeat his greatest opponent, death itself, and insisted that Clenned reveal the secret. The monk politely refused, remarking that the High King of Ireland surely had all the riches he needed. Finlith grew angry and threatened to end the monk's life unless he revealed his knowledge to him.

Clenned relented and told the king to follow his instructions. He commanded Finlith to swim in the local cesspit at sunrise every morning, then drink a cup of his own urine mixed with nettles and sheep dung at sunset. Although disgusting, the monk explained that if the king could commit to these actions for a whole year, the gift of eternal life would be his. Clenned would return a year to the day to ensure Finlith had completed his task and prove the outcome.

The king carried out the monk's instructions to the letter. Day after day, he took an early morning dip in the foul-smelling latrine and finished it by peeing into a cup and downing the result. The king's odour soon became unbearable, and even his wife started to avoid him. Finlith carried on with the revolting routine, confident in the knowledge that his reward was coming,

True to his word, Clenned returned a year to the day since his last visit and knelt before Finlith and the entire court. The king asked the monk greedily whether immortality was finally his, to which the monk replied yes if he accepted Christ as his true saviour. The confused king assured the monk that he had done everything he asked. The monk retorted that eternal life was given only to those who entered the kingdom of heaven. No one here on earth could buy that gift, especially not someone stupid and vain enough to bathe in shit and drink their own wee.

The court laughed at the king for falling victim to the prank, and Finlith was enraged. Furious at his public humiliation, he demanded that the monk be dragged from his sight and put to death at once. Clenned accepted the judgement with a smile and remarked that he would gladly enter heaven, as only there would he no longer be able to smell the king's stench. This caused another burst of laughter from the court as guards escorted Clenned from the throne room.

The monk was tied in chains and thrown into the Irish Sea, where he was said to have miraculously floated out on the tide and disappeared over the horizon.

The king, however, could not live down the embarrassment of being known as 'piss-breath' in Gaelic, and soon enough, new pretenders for the throne emerged. Finlith was killed in battle, and the title of High King of Ireland passed on to another. It seems he wasn't immortal after all, as the title of 'piss-breath' has been handed down through the ages and is now held by Bear Grylls.

The Original Statue of Liberty That Everyone Hated

The Statue of Liberty is one of the most iconic statues in the world. The 150-foot-tall Lady Liberty standing over New York harbour was a gift from France in 1886 and has been cherished by Americans ever since. The original present received a very different welcome.

The idea of giving America a statue of friendship came about years earlier and found immediate support among the French public, who donated money to its construction through a Gallic crowdfunder. A competition was held to decide on the statue, with architects across France presenting their ideas. Architect Frederic Bartholdi submitted his now-famous design of a classically inspired figure holding a torch, which was the clear favourite.

Anton Dupont was a rubbish designer with terrible taste. His most famous creation was a hideous statue of Napoleon III that he had built in Paris to honour the French leader. It was so grotesque, resembling a deformed gargoyle from the Notre Dame cathedral, that Dupont was imprisoned for two weeks as punishment.

So, when the untalented Frenchman threw his Gallic hat into the ring, he seemed unlikely to win the competition. He did have one thing going for him – he was stinking rich and not above a bit of bribery. To people's shock, the judges announced his design as the winner.

So, work got underway on Dupont's creation. The building of the statue took three years before being shipped across the Atlantic to be fully assembled on Liberty Island. At the grand unveiling, hundreds of New Yorkers, including prominent politicians and high-society folk, gathered at the base to witness it. When the giant covering was pulled away, the audience gasped in shock. Several men and women fainted, including the Major of New York. Dupont's statue portrayed a giant eagle with the Declaration of Independence in its mouth and Uncle Sam riding on its back. In short, the statue was hideous, and boos quickly broke out from the horrified crowd. Luckily Dupont wasn't there for the ceremony – otherwise, the public would have lynched him.

Rather than an eagle, many remarked that the statue looked more like a malnourished turkey with newspaper stuffed in its mouth, and the figure of Uncle Sam resembled a poor vagrant in a top hat clinging to its feathers. The gift was a horrid eyesore, and the citizens of New York took it as a grave insult by the French. Rioters ransacked bakeries, and French cheeses were thrown into bonfires across the city, giving off an unpleasant odour that clung to the buildings. A gang of dock workers tried to bring the statue down using dynamite, only succeeding in knocking off the beak, which made the sight even worse.

The statue's fate soon became a diplomatic incident as complaints were heard in Congress with a motion proposed to ban Anton Dupont from America for life. In response to the criticism, Dupont remarked that his design was a true work of art and that any Americans who disapproved were simply 'imbeciles', which just fanned the flames further.

The situation was so embarrassing for both America and France that neither government could return the statue without losing face. Like someone returning a present they didn't like, Washington politely suggested that Paris take the statue back because it was so beautiful it should be seen in its home country, while the French insisted it was a gift and should remain as such.

Luckily nature finally came to the rescue. A month after the unveiling, a storm hit New York, and strong winds buffeted the statue. The design of a bird with such a massive wingspan was a particularly bad choice in the face of the elements. Sure enough, in the middle of the night, New Yorkers heard a giant crash as the statue was swept from its base and sank to the bottom of the Hudson River.

With the statue now firmly out of the picture, the French willingly agreed to replace it, much to Dupont's indignation. They picked the runner-up from the competition to speed up the process; Bartholdi's Statue of Liberty, which was hurriedly built and shipped over to replace its previous tenant on Liberty Island. The new statue received a rapturous welcome, and New Yorkers took it to their hearts, while Dupont's creation was salvaged from the harbour and sold for scrap. The French architect never had a design commissioned again, although he managed to get hold of the giant top hat from the statue, which he kept in his garden.

The Rival Inventor Who Prank-Called Alexander Graham Bell

Scotsman Alexander Graham Bell is a historic inventor known to the world as the creator of the first telephone.

Numerous rivals were working on the concept, but the US-based Bell successfully patented his invention ahead of them on 7 March 1876. Despite his victory, there was controversy over how the wily Scotsman had managed to win the race. There were suspicions that he had used underhand tactics, stealing ideas from his rivals, and using his contacts in the patent office to push ahead in the queue. One rival inventor, Kendrick McGill, took losing out to Bell to heart and was determined to get his own back.

The victorious Scotsman founded the Graham Bell telephone company, which soon made serious money. Bell installed telephone wires across northwest America and sold telephones to those wealthy enough to afford them. And, of course, a phone took pride of place in his own home.

Here Kendrick McGill saw his opportunity for revenge. Getting Bell's home number from an associate, he made the first prank call in history. He started ringing his rival's telephone and hanging up straight away.

Assuming there must be a glitch, Bell demanded that all the house wiring be replaced. However, the problem kept happening for weeks on end. McGill took to ringing in the middle of the night and saying random words like 'banana', 'toilet seat', and 'hullabaloo'. A confused Bell became increasingly irate that his telephone system seemed to be cutting in and out.

McGill was enjoying winding up his rival and went even further. After drinking too much one night, he rang up the Bell household and started cursing down the phone. Bell finally realised he had an adversary but couldn't work out who it was. Only a hundred people owned a telephone and calling 1471 wasn't an option.

McGill grew even bolder and would goad Bell, telling the inventor that he had poor personal hygiene and rubbish dress sense. Bell angrily demanded that the prankster reveal himself, to which McGill would laughingly hang up. Things got so bad that the humiliated Scotsman refused to pick up his creation for fear of being insulted further. He instructed his long-suffering wife to answer any callers and tell them he was out.

In the end, McGill was unmasked thanks to his telephone company. His family had only learned what their husband and father was getting up to in the basement of the house when their bill arrived. It was hefty, running into many hundreds of dollars. His wife was shocked at the cost, which threatened to bankrupt them. Realising her husband's obsession with the phone calls, she went to the authorities. Following a short investigation, the police revealed her husband as Bell's tormentor.

Alexander Graham Bell wanted McGill arrested, although technically, he hadn't broken any laws, and there was no recorded evidence that he'd said anything offensive. When he took McGill to civil court, it became clear to the judge that the defendant was mentally unwell. McGill's behaviour became increasingly extreme after his case was dismissed. Eventually, he was committed to an asylum where he spent all day talking on his phone, even though there was no one on the other end.

Artists, Musicians, and Writers

The First Boy Band in History

Pop groups performing for hordes of screaming fans seem like a very modern phenomenon, and yet the first group was created a thousand years before BTS arrived on the scene. Funnily enough, it happened in Korea. The band in question were a group of teenage Buddhist monks from a local monastery during the Goryeo dynasty of Korea around 1050 AD. The boy's melodic chanting of Buddhist mantras and scripture was considered so heavenly it was said that the face of the Buddha would appear in the minds of enraptured listeners.

Accounts of the monk's singing spread beyond the monastery's walls, and townsfolk would travel miles to hear the group. The monastery's abbot realised he had a singing sensation on his hands and appointed himself their manager. He suggested they visit other monasteries in the region, and soon, the boys were on tour. Their fame grew as they travelled across Korea, and large crowds (often featuring lots of young women) would flock to see them.

Their popularity saw them outgrow the monastery circuit, and that summer, they performed large-scale open-air concerts – the Glastonbury and Latitude Festivals of their day. There were crushes at the front as eager fans pushed forward, and merchandise was sold in the form of wood-carved scripture from the group's lyrics. Their fame grew so great they were invited to perform in front of the emperor and his court.

The constant touring was taking its toll. The abbot tightly controlled every part of the monks' schedule as they travelled from show to show. The monks were paid nothing for their efforts and had to endure a rickety cart journey to each gig. It eventually came to light that the abbot was pocketing the profits from the merchandise and taking advantage of the group's female fans. Horrified by this behaviour, the monks wanted to fire their manager, but their religious vows meant they couldn't lift a finger. Luckily a promoter and part-time circus owner offered to help them out of their predicament. He had the abbot tied to the back of a camel and dragged through the town until he agreed to release the group.

Under new management, the boys went on an even more successful tour featuring lions, tigers, and elephants during the interval. Now the group were being paid for their talents and travelled in a sumptuous caravan stuffed with cushions and silks. The tour went international when they visited neighbours China and

Japan, where the curious Korean outfit caused quite a stir. The monkish boy band had become the biggest thing in Korea. There were said to be more shrines of them in people's homes than the emperor himself!

Cracks were starting to appear. One of the monks, Jang-Cheo, was considered the group's best singer and would often step forward to perform solo chants to captivate the crowd. As his profile increased, so did his ego, and soon he imagined himself as a solo star without the other monks holding him back. Jan-Cheo shockingly announced that he was going solo and went on his own tour. The other monks carried on without their former bandmates, forcing fans to choose between them. Sometimes Jang-Cheo and his ex-band would perform in the same town on the same day, leading to fights between their supporters, resulting in black eyes and broken noses.

As the two outfits battled for attention, a new danger appeared – a brother and sister double-act who played the flute. Their father had seen the monks' success and wanted a piece of the action. The gimmick of siblings plus woodwind proved hugely popular, and that summer, the duo was invited to appear in front of the emperor. The monks failed to receive their usual invitation, leaving them in the cold.

Finding themselves out of favour, the only thing left for the monks was a reunion tour, and they soon announced that they would be getting back together. The news hit Korea like a thunderclap – the population went wild. It seemed like they would be back on top. Then disaster struck. The Mongol hordes invaded Korea. The monks fled back to their monastery, and their voices had broken by the time the threat had passed. The teenage singing sensation was over, and they spent the rest of their days in quiet prayer and meditation.

The Murderer Who Sang on a
Cruise Ship

Crazed killers often go on the run from the authorities.
Very few of them end up singing big-band numbers on
a Caribbean cruise.

Ricardo Perez was born in Miami in 1930 after his
family moved from Cuba. The young Ricardo grew up
a troubled youth with sinister impulses but learned to
hide them behind a smiley facade and boyish good
looks. Throughout his twenties, Ricardo found it hard
to hold down a job, and in 1954 he started working at
a Florida nursing home. During the four years he
worked there, several residents passed away in their
sleep, and no one seemed to notice the pattern.

Eventually, after one elderly lady was found dead
with bruising around her neck and several heirlooms
missing, suspicion fell on the staff, particularly Ricardo. With the police closing in, Ricardo vanished
overnight. Police searched the whole of Florida but
couldn't track him down.

He had escaped by buying a last-minute ticket on a
Caribbean cruise under the assumed name of Danny

Alonso. The cruise ship was a five-star liner with a swimming pool, cocktail lounge, and live swing band performing night after night. Ricardo, or Danny, paid for the cruise by pawning the heirlooms he had hastily swiped.

Despite being on the run, Ricardo refused to keep his head down. In the middle of the two-week cruise, the band's lead singer fell ill with food poisoning, and the ever-helpful 'Danny' offered to step in.

One of his many talents was singing; he became an instant hit with passengers and crew alike. The 'Spanish Sinatra', as he came to be known, could master any song – from crooning ballads to up-tempo swing numbers – and he was offered the job full-time when the cruise was finished. Danny jumped at the chance and spent the next eighteen months travelling the warm waters of the Caribbean in style.

He was friendly with everyone on board and even managed to dine at the captain's table, although he rarely talked about his life on land and always tried to change the subject. It was the elderly passengers, of which there were very many, that Danny bonded with.

A number of these passengers, often the wealthiest, started disappearing. It was thought that they had fallen overboard in the middle of the night, and no further questions were asked. Other passengers began going missing while the ship was docked in the Caribbean, leading the crew to believe they had gone

AWOL. Then several more were discovered dead in their cabins. As the warning signs increased, the cruise company was determined to maintain its five-star image, so these incidents were kept out of the headlines.

Meanwhile, the trail had gone cold in the search for Ricardo Perez in Miami. It had been a year and a half since Ricardo had disappeared, and it seemed he would never be found until luck played a part. A secretary from the Miami Police Department decided to spend Christmas on a relaxing Caribbean cruise and returned with plenty of holiday photos. She brought the snaps into her office and handed them out. Her boss spotted a familiar face in the background, wearing a tuxedo, holding a cigar, and belting out a swing number at the top of his lungs. It was Ricardo Perez.

After learning more about the mysterious singer and the strange disappearances onboard, the police were sure they had their man. The ship was headed for the Bahamas, and so the police quickly gave chase, boarding the vessel one evening. Realising what was happening, Ricardo fled from the stage halfway through a rendition of 'My Way' and escaped through the kitchen. As the police searched every inch of the boat, Ricardo managed to steal a lifeboat and attempted to sail to the safety of the Bahamas. Unfortunately, a storm hit the Caribbean that night, and a few days later, the boat's wreck washed ashore. Ricardo's body was never found, and the police were eventually forced to close the case on the Caribbean Cruise Killer. Rumours persist that this was Ricardo's final trick and that 'Danny Alonso' lived out the rest of his days in a tropical paradise, humming songs from his cruise ship days.

The Very First Dick Pic

The penis has always been a tricky subject to capture.

Since the invention of mobile phones, over a billion pixelated genitalia have been circulated around the globe, to reactions of wonder, disgust, and laughter. The first dick pic was sent over a hundred years ago. In 1882 to be exact. And it wasn't a photo; it was a painting.

Charles Lumont was a painter from Antwerp in Belgium. He had received very little success in his early career and was reduced to eking out a living doing caricatures of tourists in the town square.

Lumont was a passionate young man who embarked on an intense relationship with the daughter of a wealthy councilman. His low status as a struggling artist meant the affair had to be conducted secretly without her family knowing. A typhoid epidemic descended on Antwerp, and the pair could not see each other. Instead, love letters were sent between the two via one of the girl's family servants.

Over time, the letters became steamier until Lumont could no longer contain himself. His lover had requested that Charles paint her a self-portrait as a keepsake. In his 'eager' state, he decided to go one step further. Flinging his clothes to the floor of his dingy studio Lumont picked up his easel and produced a vivid rendering of his erect member. He then packaged the gift and addressed it to his sweetheart's house.

Unfortunately, the servant who passed on the letters had succumbed to typhoid, so her replacement received the package. She proceeded to unwrap the painting herself and let out an almighty shriek that brought the whole house running. The councilman and his wife were horrified by the offending portrait, and their daughter was forced to admit who was behind the work.

When faced with the accusation, Lumont proudly admitted to what he had done, although the fact that the picture was such an accurate rendering meant he was bang to rights anyway. The incident scandalised Antwerp: the councilman had Lumont imprisoned for public indecency, leaving the artist penniless and abandoned.

And yet it was the dick pic that came to his rescue. Despite the supposed public outrage, it turned out that many of the townsfolk wanted to look at the controversial painting. After being rescued from destruction, the artwork was put on view at a local art gallery. It soon became a sell-out attraction as crowds flocked from across Belgium to view Lumont's creation:

curiously, far more women than men queued up to take a peek.

The notorious picture was placed behind a special curtain which cost ten Francs to view. By all accounts, the painting was an accurate rendering – the Mona Lisa of the male appendage. It was even said to follow you around the room! Several people fainted, and at least one attempt was made to bless the picture with holy water.

With the exhibition proving so popular, Lumont could afford bail, and eventually, the charges were dropped.

Charles became a successful artist off the back of the controversy, and his work was soon in high demand. Although he and his partner went their separate ways, it was rumoured that he sent her a charcoal replica of the infamous painting during his time in prison, which she kept for the rest of her life.

Several years later, the original was exhibited again, but a gang of protesting clerics broke into the gallery and tried to set it on fire. The work was considered lost until it turned up in the attic of a Belgian family eighty years later. Now the painting is under lock and key in the Antwerp Museum of Art. Although Charles Lumont is now long dead, his penis still has life in it as a 'still life'.

The Actor Who Beat Up Shakespeare

William Shakespeare is one of history's greatest play-wrights, and many actors consider it the highest honour of their professional lives to perform one of his plays. An exception to this was Sir Thomas Crisp, who once punched Shakespeare in the face.

Crisp was a sixteenth-century actor with an ego. Considered one of the finest thespians of his generation, Sir Thomas performed as part of The Chamberlain's Men, a company of actors that Shakespeare wrote for. He joined the group in 1595 and performed in countless plays, including *Romeo and Juliet*, *As You Like It* and *A Midsummer Night's Dream*. As Shakespeare's reputation grew, audiences flocked to the newly built Globe Theatre in London to watch the actors strut their stuff.

Most performers would be delighted with this opportunity. Crisp hated it. He thought the Bard's plays were rubbish and only performed them for the money. He considered the material popular but flimsy trash that would be forgotten in no time. The fact he was a failed playwright may have coloured his thinking.

His opinions might have been okay if Sir Thomas had kept them to himself. However, the pompous actor made his feelings perfectly clear. The theatrical world at that time was fuelled by alcohol, and after each performance (and rehearsal), the entire company would retire to London's many taverns for a serious drinking session. Late into the night, Crisp would hector Shakespeare to his face, telling him that his plays weren't any good and listing all the ways he would improve them. His drunken suggestions included *Hamlet* being re-written as a comedy, Julius Caesar killing Brutus and setting the *Merchant of Venice* in Ipswich.

Shakespeare usually managed to humour this behaviour because Crisp was such a good actor. One night the relationship reached the breaking point. Retiring to The Crooked Swan after a flat performance of *Twelfth Night*, Sir Thomas unloaded on the playwright about his latest work, calling it 'boring beyond belief'. Shakespeare finally snapped and dumped his entire pint over his leading man, to which the offended Crisp punched him square in the face.

This kicked off a drunken fist fight, with patrons in uproar and tables flying everywhere as the two men wrestled each other to the floor. Shakespeare managed to get Crisp in a headlock, only for the actor to slip out of it thanks to the grease paint he was wearing. Crisp pulled a dagger from his jerkin and stabbed Shakespeare in the back. To the onlooker's relief, it was a prop weapon from the play. It seemed the pen was indeed mightier than the sword as Shakespeare's quill blinded Crisp in one eye while the veteran actor tugged hard on his beard. The fight spilt out of the pub and onto the street outside. A crowd of actors and drinkers followed the brawl as it descended along Fish Street onto London Bridge. Crisp took a full chamber pot of pee smashed over his head and seemed out for the count. Shakespeare walked away in triumph. Then Sir Thomas snuck up behind the playwright and pushed him into the Thames. The Bard was only saved from drowning by his colossal ruff, which acted as a life ring.

The next day Shakespeare arrived at the Globe Theatre sporting a black eye, and Crisp failed to appear for that evening's performance. The two men refused to work together again, and Sir Thomas' role was speedily re-cast. The haughty actor left London and took to performing around the country. Over the years, Crisp came to regret his decision. Conditions in the regions were harsh for touring actors, and the pampered star realised how fortunate he had been in the capital.

A decade later, he returned to London, and the two men patched up their differences. As a peace offering, Shakespeare gave Crisp the lead role in his new play, *The Tempest*, and the two retired to the pub afterwards.

Crisp still couldn't help himself and suggested several re-writes, including adding a sexy love interest for Prospero, and Shakespeare laughed it off.

As a further addition, The Globe burnt down the following year during a performance of *Henry VIII*. The source of the fire was never found, although it was rumoured that Crisp was smoking a pipe backstage and forgot to extinguish it when late for his soliloquy.

When Shakespeare died a few years later, Crisp gave the oration at his funeral, calling him 'the greatest man to have ever lived'. Of course, the actor failed to recall the time he punched him in the face and chucked him in the Thames.

The Twenty-Stone Ballet Dancer

Ballet dancers are considered graceful and athletic – the ultimate physical specimen. Lorenzo Varriano was a dancer with a difference.

Born in Italy in 1815, the nimble and slight Lorenzo exhibited talent from a young age and enrolled in Milan's world-famous La Scala ballet company. Lorenzo trained in the art of the ballerino, the lead male ballet dancer. His teachers quickly recognised his prodigious artistry, and his first public performance at fifteen drew a standing ovation from the enraptured audience. Lorenzo became a must-see attraction, and his bright future as the leading light of Italian ballet seemed assured.

By the age of eighteen, Lorenzo had started to gain weight. At first, his teachers suspected he was secretly snacking on food and the superstar teenager was punished for filling out his leotard a little too much. Despite his continued denials, Lorenzo kept gaining weight. The unfortunate truth was that Lorenzo had an overactive pituitary gland and would continue to put on weight no matter how hard he tried to stay slim.

Although upset about his condition Lorenzo was passionate about his ballet and continued to dance, ignoring the sniggers from the back of the theatre. However, La Scala was increasingly embarrassed by the ongoing situation. After he put on even more weight, the theatre company tried to fire Lorenzo, saying he wasn't punctual enough. When Lorenzo pointed out that he had never been late in his life, the theatre changed its story and claimed that his personal odour was attracting complaints from fellow dancers. When everyone signed a letter saying they had never had a problem with Lorenzo's smell, the company gave up looking for an excuse and sacked him on the spot.

The Italian public received the news with uproar. Despite criticism from a small minority of critics, ballet audiences admired Lorenzo's attitude and enjoyed his performances enormously. A boycott was organised, and crowds protested outside the ballet theatre until La Scala performed a humiliating U-turn and welcomed the return of their former leading man.

Despite his growing weight, Lorenzo entertained audiences for many more years. Although unable to perform the grander leaps and pirouettes of his contemporaries, Lorenzo's balletic movements were still said to bring tears to the eyes of onlookers. They even designed a springboard device in the wings so Lorenzo could make a dramatic entrance onstage, with a strategically placed crash mat disguised as a Renaissance bed to break his fall. Like Elvis in the 1970s, he took rest breaks during his performances to catch his breath and acknowledge the crowd while admirers swarmed to the front of the stage to grab the handkerchiefs he used to wipe sweat from his brow.

He even performed parts of his shows sitting on a stool or leaning against the set design. But despite his shape, Lorenzo still had his strength and could hold the prima ballerina of the day high in the air when they danced their pas de deux.

Eventually, by age thirty-five, Lorenzo's weight which had reached twenty-stone, had taken a considerable toll on his joints, forcing him to retire. The Italian prime minister and the entire government were in attendance for his final show, alongside the great and good of Italian society. The standing ovation lasted forty-five minutes, and the stage was covered in red roses a foot deep.

After retiring, Lorenzo became a ballet teacher with La Scala and eventually rose through the company ranks to become Director. Under his leadership, the theatre became renowned for welcoming talent from all backgrounds; how things had changed from when an overly large Lorenzo was shown the door.

Sports

The High Jumper Who Escaped from the Nazis

Jurgen Klammer was a champion German high jumper who won a silver medal at the 1936 Berlin Olympics. The Nazi regime fully embraced his success, and Klammer was invited to front a nationwide fitness programme to improve the health of the German youth. A statue was erected of him in his hometown of Hesselberg, and images of the anatomically perfect Aryan athlete were plastered across the Reich.

With the outbreak of World War Two, Klammer was given a senior role overseeing fitness in the German Army. In fact, the Olympic athlete had taken on a much more important but secret position. A Roman Catholic by faith, Jurgen and his family vehemently opposed the war and now sought to help those persecuted by the Nazis. Using his celebrity status Klammer was able to help Jews and other persecuted groups flee the country.

By 1942 the authorities had gotten wind of their activities, and the family quickly escaped abroad, except Jurgen, who bravely volunteered to stay hidden and continue the work. Eventually, the most famous high jumper in Germany was recognised and arrested. Hitler was furious at this perceived betrayal and demanded that Klammer's statue in Hesselberg be crushed into gravel. Pleas from foreign governments to let the athlete emigrate were rejected, and Klammer languished in prison.

By 1944 his continued imprisonment was becoming too much of an embarrassment, and plans were made to send Klammer to a concentration camp. Luckily the sports star was given advance warning thanks to a friendly prison guard and had time to plot his escape. The day before being transferred, Klammer requested he be allowed to stretch his legs in the prison yard. The guards overlooked his warm-ups beforehand and didn't ask why he wore shorts in February. Putting his high jump skills to maximum use, Klammer vaulted over the prison walls and escaped.

A local family hid the fugitive for a few days before smuggling him to the Swiss border. Klammer gave away his Olympic silver medal to bribe the border guards, which he had managed to keep hidden since his arrest. After crossing into Switzerland, he travelled to the US and reunited with his family. When the war finished, it was assumed that Klammer would seek American citizenship, but instead, he returned to West Germany as a hero. He opened a high jump school for Olympic hopefuls and saw a new statue unveiled at a ceremony in Hesselberg. There the tearful German was handed back his silver medal.

The Only Murderer to Win a Gold Medal

Killing someone usually leads to a prison sentence or even the death penalty. In 1912 it was rewarded with an Olympic gold medal. It featured a Hungarian discus thrower, Lestor Varga, who represented his country at the Stockholm games. Varga was a burly figure and considered the clear favourite in the contest. Then on the day of the competition, tragedy struck.

Lestor's first two throws were worryingly below par. Going into his final attempt, the Hungarian athlete was in second place, a few centimetres behind his Greek rival. The Hungarian had to make his last throw count. Taking an extra-long run-up, Lestor shut his eyes tightly and hurled his discus through the air with the last of his strength. At that exact moment, an unfortunate press photographer looking for a toilet took a shortcut across the field. Lestor's discus struck him despite shouts from onlookers, and he collapsed to the turf.

The throw wouldn't have placed Lestor first, but it bounced off the poor man's head and landed ten centimetres further down the field. Lestor had set a new world record, and the place was in uproar. Lestor's discus killed the photographer outright, and Greece demanded that he be kicked out of the competition. But when officials went through the Olympic rule book, they found nothing to prevent the attempt from standing, and there was no penalty for killing anyone. And so Lestor was an Olympic champion.

The Swedish authorities felt differently and charged the discus thrower with murder. Lester stood on the Olympic podium while handcuffed to a Swedish policeman until the Hungarian national anthem finished, and he was led away. Lestor was later found guilty of manslaughter and sentenced to ten years in prison, but a diplomatic deal saw him returned to Hungary. Thousands of people were there in Budapest to greet their gold medal winner, conveniently ignoring the death that came with it.

The Olympic committee changed their rules for the following games so this morbid incident could not be repeated. Lestor was determined to win another medal. However, the First World War brought things to a halt. The next Olympic games didn't take place until 1920, and by then, Hungary had been banned along with Germany and Austria. Greece won the discus gold medal in his absence and set a new world record.

Hungary was readmitted for the 1924 Olympics in Paris, and, despite ill health and alcoholism, Lestor vowed to take his title back. Taking in the sights of the Eiffel Tower the day before the competition, Lestor chose to climb all 650 steps to the top. There he suffered a massive heart attack and died. For the second time, he returned to Budapest to be welcomed by huge crowds. Ten men had to carry his coffin as he was buried with his gold medal and extra-heavy discus.

The Shipwrecked Crew That Invented Swingball

Swingball is a popular summer game, usually played in the back garden with a BBQ, a glass of Pimms, and a gaggle of noisy children. The origins of the game are quite different.

In 1778 a Dutch East India Company ship was sailing across the Indian Ocean when a typhoon caused it to capsize. The ship's captain Erik Van Stroos and crew were shipwrecked on a nearby tropical island. Captain Von Stroos hoped they'd soon be rescued with the island close to shipping routes, but after several weeks, they had seen nothing on the horizon.

While they could scavenge food and water from the island, the captain recognised that exercise would be vital in keeping his crew physically and mentally healthy. However, the crowded jungle and rocky beaches restricted how much activity the men could do. Instead, Van Stroos devised a game using a hollow coconut hung from a palm tree with twine salvaged from the wreck, and thus the tropical version of swingball was invented.

Paddles were fashioned from pressed coconut leaves, and the crew used the game to maintain their physical fitness and brain power. Captain Van Stroos had the men play swingball every day of the week, apart from Sunday, when they rested for prayer. Competitions were created with the winner receiving extra rations and a crown of seashells to be worn by the victor. The crown was highly sought after, so games could get quite fierce, resulting in bruised faces and missing teeth.

After eighteen months of hard-core swingball, the crew were finally rescued by a passing ship and returned home to Holland. News of their remarkable survival travelled across Europe, and people were curious to see the game themselves. And so, Van Stroos and his crew toured the continent playing exhibition matches.

The high point of the swingball tour was a game played with Louis the Sixteenth in the Gardens of Versailles. The crew was instructed to let the French monarch win. However, one midshipman, drunk on champagne, smacked the coconut straight at the king's head, knocking his crown clean off. The royal court was shocked. The quick-thinking Van Stroos dropped to one knee and presented the king with a sea-shell crown. Louis burst into laughter.

With the royal seal of approval, the swingball craze took off in France. Voltaire, Mozart and even Benjamin

Franklin were known to play the game. Captain Van Stroos attempted to patent the invention and make money from the sport. By the time he got around to it, disaster struck. The French Revolution swept the king from power, and everything associated with the old regime, particularly fancy party games, were now out of favour,

Now infamous as the swingball inventor, Van Stroos was chased out of France and fled across the channel to England. There he tried to market his game as an anti-French weight-loss device, but Georgian society in Britain had no interest in losing weight. The bankrupt Dutchman finally admitted defeat and headed back out to sea. There his bad luck continued. He was shipwrecked for a second time while sailing across the Atlantic. This time, Van Stroos had no interest in coming up with exciting new games and just sat on the beach staring at the horizon. When he was rescued months later, the Dutch captain had gone mad. If only he had played swingball himself.

The Game of Chess on Mount Everest

Reaching the summit of Mount Everest pushes you to the limits of human endurance. With only a third of the oxygen available at sea level, summiting the mountain means entering the 'death zone', the altitude at which your body is quite literally dying. Speed is crucial – get up and down as quickly as possible. That is unless you're the American twins who played a game of chess at the top of the world.

Dana and Bradley Reagan were competitive siblings with a passion for mountain climbing. By age twenty-five, they had conquered most European peaks, including the Matterhorn and the Eiger. They would bicker and argue their way up the mountain face, only to hug it out when they got back down. While drinking one night, Dana suggested they give Mount Everest a shot. Bradley thought it so unlikely that he agreed on one condition; if they both made it to the top, they would play each other at chess.

And so, they played chess at 29,000 feet, a new world record. Bradley brought the board under his thermals while Dana stuffed the pieces in her socks. They played a game for half an hour, which must have been confusing for fellow climbers reaching the summit. They must have thought their oxygen canisters were broken and that they were hallucinating.

And who won the match? Bradley took Dana's rook and put her king in check at a crucial moment. Furious at finding herself losing, Dana responded by knocking her king off the board, where it promptly plummeted 5,000 feet down the north face into China. Having lost her crucial piece, Dana was forced to concede. The two returned safely, although Bradley gloated all the way down the mountain. Somewhere at the foot of Everest is the missing chess piece. Unfortunately, it's unlikely to be found – as it's white.

The Female Boxer Who Won the Men's Heavyweight Title

In nineteenth-century England, bare-knuckle boxing was the most popular sport in the country. Thousands of eager spectators would cheer on the pugilists as they boxed round after round until one lay battered and bleeding on the sawdust floor.

There was only one thing not allowed anywhere near the ring, and that was women. Females were considered far too dainty to watch the gruesome proceedings, and there was no question of them taking part. That is until one woman managed to sneak her way into the ring.

Roisin Green was an Irish immigrant living in the East End of London in the 1860s. She came from a long line of bare-knuckle boxers from Belfast, and fighting was in her blood. Her father Gerry was a champion boxer back in his day and had held several unofficial titles from the homeland. Roisin was a chip off the old block. She proved her fighting credentials from an early age, knocking down teenage boys in the alleys of

Limehouse until she developed such a reputation that none of them would go near her.

By age eighteen, Roisin was itching to get into the ring and have a go against her male counterparts. The idea was laughed at. So, she hit upon a novel idea – she would disguise herself as a bloke. At six feet tall and with a broad figure, Roisin figured she could get away with it. Sporting outfits at that time were pretty substantial, so she could tape down her figure and tie up her auburn hair under a peaked cap. With her look now complete, no one would suspect that this broad-hipped, fresh-faced youth named 'Rian' was a woman.

To get started, Roisin bribed entry into her first match, a dingy affair in Poplar. She went six rounds before defeating her opponent, an alcoholic candle-maker named Reggie Coombes. The victory led to more opportunities, and Roisin was soon pocketing her winnings every weekend. During the day, she worked in a sewing factory and would come into work on Monday morning sporting an assortment of cuts and bruises. As an excuse, she blamed the marks on a drunken boyfriend, and the sad fact was no one else blinked an eye.

After several low-level knockouts, she was booked to enter the big Saturday night bout in New Cross. The boxing was a level above what Roisin expected, and she narrowly lost to a Slovenian welder. But in the crowd that night was her dad Gerry, who thought he recognised something peculiar about the pale skinned 'Rian' who fought like a tiger. Sneaking backstage afterwards, he found his daughter with a frozen lamb chop to her swollen face and discovered the truth.

Gerry was furious but recognised her talent and agreed to train her so she could go even further. He worked with Roisin in secret, using the tricks he had picked up from his years in boxing. She filled her mouth with tobacco as a mouthguard and soaked her hands in brandy to toughen them up.

The results paid off, and Rosin started rising through the boxing ranks. For the next two years, she boxed her way around the country, making a name for herself as the 'Irish Pixie', so called because of her feminine appearance. The high point of her career came in 1868 in a field outside Birmingham, where she defeated the renowned Tommy 'Ironface' Johnson to win the heavyweight title. The victory by an Irish immigrant was celebrated in tenements across the country, with no one suspecting there was an even more remarkable achievement behind the story.

With new fame came business opportunities, and 'Rian' was offered money to advertise a whole host of men's products – pantaloons, eau de toilette, and even shaving cream. Her picture was sold for a farthing, and a special box was constructed for her next fight so that members of the royal family could come and watch.

This level of fame brought new scrutiny. 'Rian' and her trainer insisted that no one be allowed to visit the boxer immediately before or after a fight, which fuelled suspicions of cheating. A journalist from the News of the World managed to sneak backstage hidden in a barrel of Guinness. Stinking of stout, he peered through a keyhole and discovered the secret. The next day the paper ran a front-page splash revealing that the world's heavyweight champion was a woman.

The boxing world was thrown into turmoil. Roisin was stripped of her title, which was handed over to her defeated, somewhat shame-faced opponent Tommy Johnson.

Although banned from men's boxing Roisin and Gerry refused to give up and became instrumental in founding women's boxing. Roisin founded the first women-only boxing club and toured the country, arranging matches and meeting a growing army of female fans who saw her as an icon. She even agreed to be studied by anatomists from the University of Oxford, fascinated by how the supposed 'weaker sex' was able to defeat her male opponents.

In 1900 the money dried up, and she emigrated to New Zealand to run a pub called 'The Ginger Fist' in honour of her brandy-soaked hands. Roisin's photo with the heavyweight belt took pride of place over the bar. Even in her 60s, Roisin was still willing to go a round for a shilling with any drunken customer who was foolhardy to insist on boxing the 'Irish Pixie'.

The Very Stupid Olympics

There have been some noteworthy Olympic games over the years, featuring arguments, boycotts, and bomb plots. The most ridiculous was the 1904 games in St Louis, Missouri. The Olympic Committee had just appointed a new President, and he had some barmy ideas for raising the fledgling competition's profile.

In an exhibition of physical strength, the 1904 Olympics saw arm wrestling entered as an official sport. Bouts took place on a trestle table in the middle of the athletics track, and games were won by playing best of nine. The competition featured a number of broken wrists and dislocated fingers, and the final had to be restarted several times after the trestle table kept collapsing. A 50-year-old Pole won the gold medal, although the result was muddied by allegations he had used his bad breath to put his opponents off.

There was also a competition for holding your breath underwater. The first round required competitors to descend to the bottom of the pool and hold their breath for a minute. Each further round then increased that threshold by another thirty seconds.

The competition attracted over fifty entrants, who simultaneously took part in the challenge. Those who came up for air were immediately disqualified. The competition proved extremely risky, and by the seventh round, several competitors had to be rescued by officials after passing out. The eventual winner was a Brazilian who held his breath for seven and a half minutes in the thirteenth round. He received his gold medal alone on the podium, as the other medal winners were being resuscitated! Luckily, they both survived and received their medals in hospital.

In athletics, a new sport was created to judge the competitor's speed and agility. Two players faced off against each other in a game of 'tag', with one having to grab a red handkerchief from the belt of the other. Games took place in a chalked-out arena filled with gymnastic obstacles, similar to modern parkour. Each player had five minutes to grab the handkerchief off their opponent before players swapped over and went again. The games proved tiresome because players had to wear full flannel suits with shirt and tie. The final saw the hosts, America take the gold ahead of Holland in a gripping match that lasted six hours. This was helped by the fact both athletes were taking cocaine powder to help them run faster.

But the stupidest sport at the Olympic games was musical statues. Each nation entered a relay team to run the 4 x 400 metres while classical music played from a gramophone through a loudspeaker. Whenever the record stopped, athletes had to come to a complete stand-still while officials observed them for the slightest movement or twitch. Any athlete who couldn't stay motionless was ejected from the race, and their country disqualified.

The spectacle descended into farce when every team in the final was eliminated, and the race had to be re-run. After trying twelve times, they were no closer to declaring a winner, and with daylight fading, they had to cancel the whole thing. The athletes adjourned to a nearby tent, where they tossed a coin to find the winner. Uruguay took the gold.

The 1904 Olympics concluded in embarrassment for the committee, and shortly afterwards, the President was ousted. Never again would musical statues grace the Olympiad.

Hobbies and Fashions

The Russian Tsar Who Invented the Escape Room

Escape rooms are the perfect activity for a team away day, helping develop crucial skills for the modern office environment, such as goal-oriented communication management. Sure, they may be slightly stressful. I mean, how many times do you need to get yelled at by Jill from HR to check behind the painting for a golden key that unlocks the safe? At least you don't die in horrible agony, choking on blood, and tripping over entrails as you evacuate your bowels.

Unfortunately, that was the fate for some who took part in the world's first escape room, cooked up by a mad tsar from medieval Russia. Boris Ilyanov was a particularly sadistic Russian ruler (and that's saying something) who ruled the kingdom in the last part of the sixteenth century. His passion for sadistic games was learned from a young age when he set fire to cats in St Basil's Cathedral and laughingly watched as the poor creatures thrashed about the altar.

Boris took to the throne at the age of twenty-two after witnessing his father, the Tsar, die of a heart attack in a brothel. The chroniclers don't say whether Boris was also participating in the festivities. The new ruler of Russia was less interested in the welfare of his kingdom and keener on having fun in the most twisted ways imaginable.

To this end, Boris designed a giant maze of escape rooms in his palace. He filled them with cryptic clues and riddles to access the next room, which could be behind paintings, furniture, and fake walls. The rooms got increasingly complicated and dangerous as players went along. Some rooms were completely upside down, while others were flooded with water or in total darkness. Others were filled with manure or had sharp spikes on the ceiling that slowly descended like an Indiana Jones film. One room was even said to unleash wild wolves on the players while they worked on a puzzle.

The escape rooms were so elaborate that players had twelve hours or more to escape. If they did finally get out, often shaking and deranged from nervous exhaustion, they were given their reward and set free. Those unable to finish in time were butchered horribly by guards, running in from hidden doors to impale the losers on swords and spears.

Players were randomly picked from the streets of Moscow and offered huge piles of gold if they managed to escape. In other instances, feudal lords who arrived at Boris' court were required to play the games to receive his approval. Those who simply refused to play were massacred on the spot, so victims usually opted to take their chances in the rooms. Some players were thrown in independently, while others were forced to participate in groups. Boris once had an entire rival family of thirty take part.

The gruesome and childish tsar would gleefully watch the exploits through peepholes in the walls, often whispering hints and suggestions to the players, sometimes helpful and sometimes not. The tsar even put his sister into the rooms when she displeased him. Luckily, she survived.

The ingenuity of the escape rooms became famous beyond Russia's borders, although no one knew how grisly they could get. The British ambassador to Russia took part in the games and declared them thoroughly entertaining. In the end, Boris went too far and killed a cultural attaché sent to the court from neighbouring Tatarstan. The Tartars were understandably aggrieved and chose to invade Muscovy. With Tartar soldiers on the city's outskirts, Boris' family decided he was too much trouble, so his sister stabbed him while he slept.

The escape rooms were preserved for a time as a macabre tourist attraction before burning down in mysterious circumstances. For years afterwards, mementoes of the infamous rooms could be found on sale – bits of furniture, door handles and even ceiling spikes

– reminders of when escape rooms had nothing to do with team away days.

The Babylonian Queen who Created Twister

Twister is considered a fun party game to play with friends after a glass of wine and some nibbles. The origins of the game are much older and much more sordid.

Queen Hepthisi was a Babylonian ruler from around 450 BC. She originally came to power as the wife of King Mathesa, but after his untimely death due to gangrene from an infected shaving cut, Hepthisi decided to seize power for herself. Despite numerous rivals for the throne, the 23-year-old queen proved to be more than a match for all of them, and the region flourished under her rule.

Her most notable fame came as a result of her considerable sexual appetite. The young queen had been married off to her aged husband at fifteen, so she decided to make up for all that lost time after he popped his clogs. The royal palace soon became a den of iniquity, and word travelled fast that unending pleasures could be realised if you gained admittance through Hepthisi's golden gates.

The bold and the beautiful from across Babylon could be found queuing outside the throne room to join the queen's harem. Athleticism and suppleness were prized most highly of all, so a game was devised to test the prowess of the applicants. Four rows of coloured circles were painted on the palace floor. There the queen would spin a wheel and call out the colour, with an accompanying instruction to place either a hand or a foot. The court would watch on as more players joined the game, contorting themselves around each other in a writhing mass of bodies.

Those who proved themselves the most dexterous and strong were allowed entry to the pleasure palace, while those who fell to the floor in failure were dragged through the streets in chains before being put to death, the laughter of the court still ringing in their ears. So, remember that next time you're playing Twister while crunching on a Twiglet.

The Canadian town that hated Pork Pies

Pork pies are considered a popular British picnic snack, a tasty combination of pastry and meat. One Canadian town hated them so much they went to war.

Originally founded as a whaling port, the small Canadian town of Fort Baker lies close to the arctic circle on the shores of the Northwest Passage. The only route to and from the town is by boat, and for several months every winter, the sea ices up and Fort Baker is cut off from civilisation.

In 1923 an unusually cold spell hit the region sooner than predicted, and the sea ice froze before the town had time to gather its winter supplies. However, it seemed their luck was in. A nearby trading ship passing through the straits became trapped in the ice, and the townspeople were able to board it, looking for supplies that could last them through the dark, cold months ahead. They came across thousands of pork pies being delivered to Canada from their hometown of Melton Mowbray in Leicestershire.

For the next four months, the unfortunate citizens had to survive on little more than pork pies. They had them for breakfast, lunch, and dinner. They fried them, boiled them, mashed them up and turned them into soup. The town stunk of pork pies. They had so many they could freeze them outside and use them as bricks for buildings. When they'd built everything they could, they used the pies for target practice and had snowball fights with them.

By spring, the town had developed a pathological hatred of pork pies. They ceremoniously hurled the remaining pies into the sea when the ice thawed. They hated them so much that the town sent an envoy to Melton Mowbray, making clear how much they detested their product. Their anger increased when they failed to hear back from the British city. They wrote to the Canadian government about their wish to secede from the Commonwealth and formally declared war on Mowbray. Fourteen men signed up for the war and set sail across the Atlantic with a mission to invade Leicestershire.

At this point, Ottawa and London had to step in. The war party was intercepted and escorted to the UK, where a delegation from Melton Mowbray agreed to meet with them and apologise for any distress caused. The invaders grudgingly accepted the gesture, and both sides were encouraged to sign a 'peace treaty' promising not to attack the other for the next hundred years. The towns were twinned together to foster greater harmony, and each year they would send a representative to shake hands with the other to ensure the bad blood didn't linger.

Fort Baker's hatred of pork pies continues to this day. If you wish someone ill luck for the coming year, you give them a pork pie with their name on it, while if you want good luck, you spit on a pork pie and hurl it into the sea.

The Barber Who Shaved Hitler and Stalin

Tobias Pfeffer was a barber to two of the most infamous dictators in history.

Born in Austria in 1905, his family moved to Germany shortly afterwards. Tobias came from a long line of family barbers, and his father quickly established a shop in the centre of Berlin. After he died, Tobias took over the small business and kept it going throughout the 1930s as the Nazis rose to power. With the coming of the Second World War, life continued much the same; people still needed their hair cut, after all. But as the bombing raids increased, things became more difficult.

With the war turned against Germany by 1945, Hitler and his closest staff retreated to his underground bunker in the centre of Berlin. Here the Fuhrer descended into madness, ranting against the army's failure and his betrayal by the German people. His appearance became so alarming that those closest to him decided that a haircut was needed to smarten him up.

So a junior officer was dispatched to search the streets of Berlin for a barber.

Most hairdressers had fled the city by now. The officer discovered Tobias and ordered him to Hitler's bunker immediately. The unfortunate barber couldn't refuse. Upon arrival, he was informed that he would be cutting the hair of the Fuhrer himself. Under the watchful eye of the SS, Tobias carefully worked his scissors around the grizzled head of the German leader, knowing that one wrong cut would see him killed. Amazingly Hitler enjoyed the results and demanded a shave as well. Tobias had to stop his hands from shaking as he ran the razorblade down the Fuhrer's neck. Feeling reinvigorated by the experience, Hitler insisted that Tobias return to the bunker frequently to cut his hair and lift his mood.

And so, Tobias became Hitler's barber and confidante during the last few months of the war. The fact he was Austrian was a bonus, and Hitler spent hours over-sharing with Tobias about his dreams and his regrets about how the war had turned out. Tobias spent so much time with Hitler that others in the bunker became jealous, and Propaganda Minister Goebbels made plans to have the nuisance barber removed. He falsely accused Tobias of being Jewish and demanded a summary execution. Just as the barber seemed out of luck, the Red Army came to the rescue, breaking through the final German defences and entering the city centre.

Realising the game was up, Hitler said his final good-byes and committed suicide, closely followed by Goebbels. In the commotion, Tobias slipped out of the bunker and escaped.

Unfortunately, his adventures weren't over. Captured by the Red Army soon after fleeing, Tobias was assumed to be a high-ranking Nazi official and narrowly avoided being shot on the spot. Protesting his innocence, he showed them his shaving bag, which included a thank-you note from Hitler. The barber was handed over to the security services, who sent him to Moscow for interrogation.

Learning that Tobias had spent hours with Hitler in his final days and weeks, the Soviet leader Joseph Stalin demanded to meet the barber in person. Having missed out on capturing the German dictator, Stalin was obsessed with his nemesis and wanted to know every little detail about him. Having escaped from the frying pan Tobias was now firmly in the fire as he sat in the Kremlin nervously answering Stalin's questions.

Tobias' hopes of returning to Germany were dashed when Stalin demanded he remain in Russia. The Soviet leader was taken with the idea of employing Hitler's former barber, so Tobias found himself trimming the moustache of yet another maniacal dictator. Although living in constant fear of Stalin's whims and with the KGB watching his every move, Tobias' new life in Moscow was better than most Soviet citizens. He was provided with a comfy apartment, and his wife was allowed to move there from Berlin.

As with Hitler, those in Stalin's court became envious of the diminutive German's access to the Soviet dictator. After increasing ill health, Stalin finally died from a stroke in 1952, and the Head of the KGB, Lavrenty Beria, attempted to seize power. Tobias was thrown into a KGB prison awaiting execution the following morning. Luckily Beria's rivals in the Politburo carried out a countercoup that saw Beria overthrown. Even then, Tobias spent another six months languishing in prison. Under the new leadership, Stalin was no longer in favour, and no one knew what to do with his former barber. He spent his days giving his fellow inmates free haircuts for protection, as well as the prison governor.

Eventually, Tobias was released from prison. The new leadership wanted to reset international relations, so the German barber and his wife were allowed to emigrate to the United States. There they settled in the peace and quiet of Massachusetts. The German opened a new barber shop and kept his fascinating past a secret, although he did add one more famous customer to his resume. In 1956 US Senator and future president John F. Kennedy popped into the shop as he needed a quick trim.

The Victorian Children Who Cleaned the White Cliffs of Dover

The year was 1851, and Britain was at the height of its imperial pomp. Queen Victoria's husband, Prince Albert, organised the Royal Exhibition to show off Britain at its very best. Helping the Prince in this task was the Queen's second cousin, the punctilious Duke of Cumberland. The duke insisted everything he encountered be spotlessly clean, down to the last blade of grass and ironed napkin.

Part of the glorious image of Rule Britannia are the white cliffs of Dover, the gleaming chalk cliff face across the Kent coastline. However, by 1851 the cliffs weren't looking their best. Rather than shiny white, the chalk face had become a distinctly muddy colour, with streaks of soil, grass, and bird poo.

This wasn't good enough for the Duke of Cumberland. While inspecting the navy in Dover harbour, the duke's pedantic eye caught sight of the dirty cliffs, and he demanded that they were cleaned in time for the

Great Exhibition. With the authority of the Queen's husband behind him, no one dared object to such a ludicrous demand, and with only weeks to go until the festival, wheels were hurriedly set in motion.

Attempts were made to clean the cliffs with water and scrubbing brushes. However, they soon found these efforts were coming to nothing. With time running out, they hit upon an alternative solution – painting the cliffs with white paint.

The biggest challenge was the sheer amount of person-power needed to paint the cliffs in time. So, they found the next best thing – child power. Luckily for the duke, Victorian Britain had oodles of cheap child labour. In a recruitment drive North Korea would be proud of, children were plucked from orphanages and workhouses across London before being packed onto the train down to the south coast. The children were enticed with the payment of a shilling a day (quite a lot of money in those days), plus the suggestion that they would meet Queen Victoria and Prince Albert when they came down to visit the finished work (they never did, of course). Complaining social workers and do-gooders were assured that the bracing sea air would do wonders for the children's physical and mental health. To this end, the children were housed in tents high above the cliffs for the mammoth operation over the coming weeks.

Surprisingly no one died in the undertaking, particularly considering health and safety weren't anyone's highest priority. The children were lowered down on makeshift benches hung from ropes at the top of the cliffs. Once they had painted their way across the chalk face, they were lowered further down until the whole section was complete, and they could move on.

Remarkably the children managed to accomplish the feat. In truth, they only painted a three-mile stretch just outside Dover. Still, upon visiting the cliffs, the duke declared himself delighted with the results and recommended that all those involved be given an extra shilling for their efforts (they weren't).

The other surprising outcome was that it did work. Onlookers remarked that the finished cliffs looked clean and white, although if you were downwind, the smell of the paint fumes, a heady mix of egg, glue and oil could be particularly nauseating. One young woman passed out while admiring the cliffs from a nearby rowing boat. Of course, the pristine scene didn't last long. A thunderstorm washed all the paint off one week later, and the sea below became a foamy, milky mass of white. By then, the duke had moved onto something new and didn't care about his white cliffs anymore.

The children who painted the cliffs were packed onto trains back to London and quickly forgotten about. To mark the death of Queen Victoria in 1902, those still alive assembled high on the cliffs above Dover for a reunion and a photograph. No one dare suggest they have another go at cleaning them.

The Craze That Saw Everyone Lose an Eye

The defeat of the Ottoman Turks at the Battle of Vienna in 1683 is considered one of the most decisive events in European history. However, some people took its celebration a little too far.

One of the great heroes to emerge from the battle was Prince Ernst von Rathoffen, who served as military governor of Vienna during the fighting. At a climactic moment, the Turks finally broke through the city walls, and only thanks to the determined efforts of Von Rathoffen were they successfully repelled. While rallying his troops, a Turkish arrow hit the Austrian Prince in the eye, but he chose to stay on the battlefield and fight until the end. Afterwards, Van Rathoffen wore a velvet eye patch to cover his missing eye, and the distinctive fashion item became a triumphant symbol of victory.

A wave of nationalist hysteria took hold of the Austro-Hapsburg empire from this point on, and those in the imperial court vied with each other to show off their jingoistic credentials. The more patriotic you appeared, the faster you rose through the ranks, and the competition was fierce. After losing out on a highly sought after position at court, one young Austrian nobleman went the ultimate step and removed his eye in honour of Van Rathoffen. The next day he appeared at the palace sporting a velvet eye patch for all to see. Not wishing to appear any less loyal, others in the court followed suit, and before long, removing one's eye became a horrifying fashion craze among the nobility. They vied with each other to be seen wearing the most outlandish eye patches, sporting leopard print, diamonds, and peacock feathers. The craze reached a crescendo when one ambitious army officer looking for promotion plucked out both eyes, ironically harming his prospects greatly.

Eventually, these incidents became too numerous to ignore, and Emperor Leopold published a royal edict banning the practice. Unfortunately, the desperate desire for status was so acute that people continued taking out their eyes, even after the emperor had told them not to. One struggling nobleman insisted that he had accidentally lost his eye after falling asleep drunk at the dinner table and landing on his knife.

To stop this macabre fad from injuring his entire nobility, the emperor threatened them all with their worst punishment. Anyone found to be missing an eye would henceforth be banned from court and their possessions confiscated. And so, the practice ceased overnight.

Instead, people across the empire were encouraged to exhibit their patriotism by wearing a symbolic eye patch without gouging out their retina. Cloth manufacturers did great business churning out the garments, while the poorest who couldn't afford an eyepatch rubbed charcoal around their eye sockets. Meanwhile, a glazed doughnut was cooked up by Viennese bakeries with a sultana plonked on top, which became affectionately known as 'Van Rathoffen's eye'.

A List of Firsts

The First Autograph Hunter

Autographs are a highly valued item, collected by fans who want to feel a connection with the celebrities they idolise. And the first autograph hunter was no different.

Spurious Felix was a Roman citizen with a passion for collecting autographs. Born in Rome in the first century AD, Spurious grew up idolising the men and women who appeared at the Circus Maximus, the huge sports stadium in the city's centre. Spurious visited the stadium each weekend and became obsessed with having a permanent memento from the charioteers, gladiators and athletes who performed there. He came up with the idea of asking them to ink their signature onto parchment or print it on a wax tablet. No one had ever done this before, and people became fascinated with Spurious' curious hobby.

Spurious went to extreme lengths to obtain his autographs. He pestered people so much that eventually, the authorities refused him access to the stadium. His solution was to dress up as a charioteer and sneak backstage. He was able to do this several times until he was mistakenly placed in an actual chariot race and almost died in a crash. He kept being banned from the Circus Maximus, but the public's goodwill meant he was repeatedly allowed back in.

By now, his passion for autographs was no longer limited to sports stars, and Spurious grabbed signatures from anyone famous in Roman life. He chased down poets, actors, and senators and even tried to get an autograph from Emperor Claudius, who was walking through the streets one day. Pushing through the crowds, he ran up to the startled emperor and was immediately surrounded by imperial bodyguards, who readied themselves to kill him. After hearing of the request, the emperor chuckled and handed Spurious his autograph, which took pride of place in his growing collection. Spurious wasn't just interested in the upper classes. When a prominent Roman prostitute became embroiled in a scandal with a famous senator, Spurious plucked up the courage to visit her brothel. He paid for her time but only asked for her autograph, to which she agreed.

After years of collecting, Spurious' house was full of autographs, and he eventually turned his home into a museum, charging the public two denarii to visit. The autographs became very sought after, and he turned down every offer to buy them.

His hankering for autographs was so great that he went abroad to France and Spain to collect them from local governors and famous soldiers. He even planned to visit the Barbarian tribal leader in Germania but was warned that his head would probably end up on a spike. Sometimes he couldn't see someone in person, so he had the idea to send them a letter by post and request they return it with their signature.

Just as autographs dominated his life, so they led to his death. When Spurious heard stories about a curious religious leader called John the Baptist living in Turkey, he was determined to get his autograph. Unfortunately, his ship sank during a storm in the Mediterranean, and Spurious drowned.

His house in Rome remained a tourist attraction for several years until it burnt down in the great fire of Emperor Nero's reign. His legacy lived on. The philosopher and writer Pliny the Elder wrote in his memoirs about the curious Roman citizen who one day appeared at his door uninvited and wouldn't leave until he received an autograph.

The World's First Roundabout

Nowadays, motoring roundabouts are considered a normal (if terminally boring) part of the UK driving experience. Back in the day, the simple roundabout blew people's minds.

The first roundabout was built in 1909 in Letchworth, Hertfordshire, and caused quite a stir. People flocked from miles around to witness its official opening by the mayor. The first road traffic accident occurred twenty minutes after its unveiling and continued at the rate of three a day. Weeks later, many motorists still distrusted the circular road system and would choose a different route to avoid the obstacle.

The roundabout became a tourist attraction, and people would gaze in wonder as cars attempted to navigate this strange construction, secretly hoping to witness a crash. The roundabout's fame grew, and companies jockeyed with each other to put up advertising hoardings around the site. Food and souvenir sellers were there to remind people about their exciting day out. A couple even decided to get married there, exchanging their vows amidst the traffic fumes.

On another occasion a family took an outing to the roundabout and decided to picnic in the middle. The problem came when they tried to leave the roundabout and found that with the evening rush hour, it was much busier than when they had arrived. The family, which included an elderly grandmother, were trapped for over an hour until the police came and closed the road, allowing them to cross back safely.

People were so keen on exploring the roundabout that they were unaware of the risks involved, and an innocent bystander was run over. From then on, the roundabout was considered off-limits to pedestrians, and safety barriers were constructed.

Eventually, roundabouts became common across the UK, and the Letchworth tourist site lost its sparkle. Nowadays, no one goes there to take photos or get married, although it still suffers the odd accident or two.

The First Joining of the Mile High Club

Francis Collingsworth was an American female aviator who made quite a name for herself. Born in 1905, she developed a passion for aeroplanes from a young age and took to flying in her teens. Collingsworth's displays of aerobatic daring captured people's imagination, and she got a job travelling across the United States, performing in touring shows at local aerodromes.

The adventurous Collingsworth was bisexual, and while stationed in Kansas, she had a passionate relationship with a female secretary who worked at the airfield. Unfortunately, the woman was married, and the clandestine affair had to be conducted in secret. With intimate moments impossible to come by on the ground, the two lovers found that the only time they could be together uninterrupted was up in the air. Francis took to giving the secretary flying lessons as a cover story, and the two lovers spent endless hours soaring through the blue skies.

But sitting alongside each other in an aircraft wasn't the only thing they were looking for. With things heating up between the pair, the impulsive Francis made her move at 12,000 feet. And so, on the 13 July 1930, the two women became the first members of the mile-high club. The exact details of the episode aren't printable. It didn't go that smoothly, as ten minutes later, a stray foot accidentally pushed on the controls, and the plane stalled before plunging into a deadly freefall. Collingsworth grappled with the joystick and recovered the flight seconds before it crashed. She managed to perform an emergency landing in a local farmer's field.

The farmer was surprised to discover a plane in his wheat field and equally shocked to find the two pilots in various stages of undress. The pair explained that their clothes had come off in the bumpy landing, but word got back to the secretary's husband that something fishy had gone on.

Faced with a messy situation, Collingsworth headed off on the next stage of her tour while her ex-lover plucked up the courage to divorce her husband and begin a whole new chapter of her life. Word grew of Francis' exploits, and eventually Hollywood came calling for the mile-high lothario, who became a hugely successful movie pilot.

The First Trainspotter

Trainspotting is a hobby that demands dedication, like hours spent in the freezing rain at Crewe waiting for a brief glimpse of the No. 925 from Cheltenham. At least nowadays you have plenty of trains to choose from. Finchley Ambrose was born in 1802 with a passion for trains, and unfortunately, there was only one for him to spot.

In the early nineteenth century, the invention of railway steam locomotives was just taking off. The first time Finchley ever saw a train was on the 12 September 1825. It was the maiden running of George Stephenson's Locomotion 1, the first steam train ever to carry passengers. It travelled along the Stockton to Darlington railway line near where Finchley lived. At that moment, he was rendered speechless by the sight of that extraordinary machine with smoke billowing from its spout, pistons whirring non-stop and an ear-shredding whoosh of noise. To Finchley, it was a religious experience.

The young man immediately became obsessed with steam trains. He would spend countless hours on the passenger wagon hauled by Locomotion up the line and then back again. When he wasn't on the train, he would wait all day to watch it pass by and then note the exact time it appeared. Soon he had reams of entries saying the same thing day after day. He would put on his woolly hat, bring out a mug of tea and stand for hours waiting for the train to arrive.

Finchley was certainly a trainspotter, but the problem was he didn't have enough trains to spot. He had to wait another four years until George Stephenson's son Robert launched his Rocket steam engine, which ran between Liverpool and Manchester. Finchley was there for its first outing and spent the whole week watching the brand-new train go back and forth.

Within a decade, many more railway lines were operating across the country, and Finchley visited each one, sometimes several times a year. His record for watching the train to Derby was over a hundred, and he took to sketching each train for his record keeping. His passion for trains gained him a reputation, and his name appeared in The Times newspaper. He was even offered a job as a coal shoveller on a train, although he was fired after only a few days because he got so excited and kept forgetting to put coal in the boiler.

Railway mania swept across Britain into the 1840s and beyond. By now, Finchley was complaining there were too many trains to choose from, and he missed the early days when all he had to watch was the

Locomotive 1 that travelled past his house. In the end, it was the trains that cost him his life. While trying to sketch a brand-new train as it passed him just outside York, he accidentally lost his footing on the rails and slipped in front of the train. The railway company paid for his funeral, and his coffin was taken home on the Stockton to Darlington railway.

The First Ever Skydive

Skydiving is a high-octane venture that requires nerves of steel. You would assume this sport only took off once aeroplanes were available, but it predates them by over thirty years.

The first skydiver was a Belgian inventor named Claude Lucille. Claude had been tinkering in his workshop on what we would now call a parachute. He was convinced that humans could fall through the air at dizzying speeds before pulling out his invention and floating safely down to earth, but he was having trouble proving it. He had tried jumping from the roof of his house in Bruges. However, the building wasn't high enough. Unfazed, Claude tried again. This time he chose the spire of St Salvator's cathedral. Sneaking up the staircase during mass, he jumped off a gargoyle. The same thing happened. Thankfully Claude landed on a hedge and only suffered a sprained ankle. He was banned for life from the church by a furious Bishop.

Claude kept going. Despite his failure, the Belgian firmly believed that the skydive would succeed if only he could try it on a much greater height. And so, in 1896, he had a risky idea.

Claude's good friend, Arthur, was a passionate balloonist, and one day Claude suggested they go up to take in the view. Pleased with Claude's eagerness, Arthur agreed, and one Saturday morning, they ascended in the wicker basket as hot air filled the balloon. Arthur did query why Claude had brought such a bulky backpack with him, and Claude explained it was for a weather experiment he was working on.

They soon reached a hundred feet above the Belgian countryside, and Claude requested they keep going. Arthur was surprised but agreed. Every five minutes Claude would propose that his increasingly reluctant friend take him even higher until they were over a thousand feet in the air. By now, there was frost on the basket, and the air was thin. They were getting dangerously high into the atmosphere. Arthur finally had enough and refused to go any higher. Turning his back on his friend, he made urgent preparations to take the balloon back down.

Claude now saw his opportunity. Arthur turned back just in time to have the shock of his life as he saw Claude clamber over the side of the basket. He went to stop his friend from jumping to certain death, but Claude uttered 'pardon' and leapt from the balloon. Arthur shrieked in horror as he watched his friend plummet into the distance.

Claude only managed to skydive for thirty seconds, but that was enough time to risk his life. Falling at such a speed, he was immediately disoriented and caught in a deadly spin. Deafened by the wind, eyes half-blinded, and limbs flailing, he was in danger of passing out. At the last possible moment, he managed to pull on the cord of his parachute, which miraculously inflated and brought his free fall to a neck-juddering halt.

Half unconscious, Claude now found himself drifting serenely to the ground. The rest of the descent took him seven minutes. He had chosen to wear two jackets to keep warm and hide a flask of whisky, which he used to revive himself. The only problem he hadn't considered was the weather. Although sunny, it was windy, and Claude was blown several miles out over the North Sea. Landing in the water, he got caught up in his parachute and would have drowned had he not been spotted by a local fisherman.

People were amazed by the endeavour. The local priest even allowed him to return to mass. Claude made three more skydives from a balloon, although Arthur refused to remain his friend. For the final jump, a local butcher sponsored him, and he clung on to a tin of meat for the duration of the descent. The extra weight sped up his fall and almost killed him, so M. Lucille retired. He never went up in a balloon again.

World Records

The Most Northerly B&B

Hotels can be found almost anywhere on Earth nowadays, from tropical jungles to the hottest deserts – plus Hemel Hempstead. If you're looking to pay for a bed, no matter where you are, you can usually find one. The most northerly hotel in the world is currently listed as the Radisson hotel on the Norwegian islands of Svalbard. The record for the most northern hotel ever goes to an Inuit named Panuk, who, in 1908, set up a B&B.

Panuk and his Inuit people lived in the coastal areas between Greenland and Canada, deep inside the arctic circle, where permanent ice covered the sea all year round. While the conditions could be harsh, the Inuit lived comfortably with their surroundings. The same couldn't be said for outsiders. Although the Inuit had dealt with European traders on the Northwest passage for many years, by the 1900s Panuk noticed strangers heading north across the ice. These were European explorers attempting to reach the North Pole, the new holy grail for Arctic exploration.

Unfortunately, they were ill-prepared for the harsh conditions they encountered, and Panuk was shocked when he stumbled across a travelling party frozen to death in the snow. Most Inuit were dismissive of these idiot strangers, but Panuk felt a pang of compassion. He decided to open a 'hotel' for them to stay in. In truth, it was a simple igloo filled with caribou hide to keep warm; to any European explorer, it was luxury.

The first explorers to use the hotel were an American party struggling through a snowstorm close to death until Panuk led them to the safety of his igloo. There they waited out the storm and, in the morning, enjoyed a hearty breakfast of herring, freshly caught by Panuk himself.

Word soon spread, and other explorers quickly used Panuk's little hotel as a resting point before going to the Pole. They offered to pay him for the bed and breakfast, but money was no good to an Inuit. In the end, they paid him in gifts, ranging from iron nails, whale blubber, and an Edwardian fashion magazine. Panuk had the pages proudly displayed on the walls of his igloo.

The popularity of Panuk's hotel wasn't always a good thing. One night the igloo was 'double-booked' when a party of Norwegians and British adventurers turned up. The rival countries were both trying to reach the pole, and each team spent the night glaring at the other from each side of the igloo. When morning came, a heated argument broke out over who would be the first to get away, almost collapsing the igloo when it came to blows. Another time the hotel was rammed full when a British party was rescued from the freezing temperatures. This included the ponies they had brought with them. Both animals and humans had to share the smelly conditions for three days until the storm lifted.

These acts of generosity didn't go unnoticed. To thank him personally for his heroics, the Royal Geographic Society issued Panuk a personal invitation to visit London for a celebratory dinner. Although advised not to go by his Inuit elders, Panuk was too intrigued by this strange land beyond the seas and hitched a ride with a returning British ship.

He arrived in London and spent the week as the most talked about person in the capital. Arthur Conan Doyle, Beatrix Potter and Winston Churchill were among the endless stream of visitors who had heard so much about this Arctic good Samaritan. The week was capped off with a fancy dinner at the Savoy, in which Panuk took his first and only sip of alcohol. He had to be carried out by the main course, which was salted herring.

However, despite their good intentions, the British had done more harm than good. Returning home, Panuk fell ill from flu, for which he had no defence and died soon after. His body was returned to his homeland,

and the igloo was abandoned. Panuk's hotel wouldn't take on any more vacancies.

The Paper Aeroplane That Flew the Furthest

Creating a paper aeroplane is something that everybody has tried. There are quite a few theories as to what makes the best design of the plane, and there are even competitions held to see how far you can get it to fly. With a sturdy creation and a good breeze, a paper aeroplane has been known to fly over 100 metres. That's nowhere near the record for the longest flight, which stands at over a million miles – and is still going strong!

The person who threw the aeroplane was NASA astronaut Gary Robertson. In 1983 he was chosen for the maiden voyage of the Challenger space programme. Challenger was a newly designed shuttle that would take off like a traditional rocket but land like an ordinary aeroplane. Gary had always had a thing for stunts during his years training as an astronaut and had something special in mind to mark the occasion of the first Challenger mission.

Unbeknownst to his superiors, Gary smuggled a piece of A4 paper aboard the flight. This may not seem like a big deal, but every item on the shuttle had to be signed off, down to the smallest nut and screw. Paper, in particular, was a no-no as it was flammable and could easily threaten the whole mission. Gary was willing to take the risk for his prank to pay off.

The shuttle launched with great success and was soon orbiting Earth. As part of the three-day mission, Gary took a spacewalk to check the ship was in working order. At this point, the rogue astronaut put his plan into action. Folding up the smuggled piece of paper to create his aeroplane, he donned his spacesuit and climbed out into the icy vacuum of space. From there, he held up the paper aeroplane. He pointed the nose out towards the blackness of the cosmos and let it go with a gentle throw. The white paper aeroplane steadily drifted away from the shuttle and was soon lost in the darkness of space.

The rest of the mission passed off without incident. When Gary returned to Earth, he revealed what he had done. NASA's top brass was furious and banned him from further missions, but his free-spirited act had won him legions of fans and admirers.

Gary's paper aeroplane has been travelling for forty years and is estimated to have flown 1.2 million miles. With no force opposing it, the plane will keep on going. Eventually, it will reach the edge of our solar system and carry on until it gets caught in the gravity of another object, and who knows where it will end up.

Gary signed the aeroplane: "Greetings from Earth!" A very curious gift from Earth to the rest of the universe.

The Quickest Bin Man

Reggie Cook was an East End bin man who plied his trade in the 1920s. It was an exhilarating time for the waste management industry. The rear-loading bin lorry had recently been invented, and bin men were becoming a staple fixture on streets up and down Britain.

Reggie wasn't just any old bin man. He claimed to be the 'quickest bin man in the world'. Despite being in his 50s, Reggie's speed, strength and agility were renowned, and it was said that he could empty the bins of a terraced street in ninety seconds flat. Cook was so good at it that people would come out of their houses each morning to watch him in action, standing in their dressing gowns and slippers as Reggie sped past them, a whirling blur of man and bin.

Whole classes of kids would be late for school on the days Reggie was doing his collections. They would cheer him on and place bets on how quickly he'd finish. He was so fixated on emptying every bin that one time, he accidentally picked up a child and threw them into the lorry. Luckily, they were rescued seconds later, although their school uniform was covered in porridge.

Reggie's exploits were covered by The Poplar Post, the local paper, and he quickly became a celebrity around London. As his fame grew, Reggie founded the 'Bin Man Olympics', a competition much like World's Strongest Man. Bin men from across the country performed remarkable feats of strength, such as carrying a bin full of water around a racecourse or seeing who could throw an empty bin the furthest. The first competition was held at Walthamstow dog racetrack, which Reggie won hands down.

Reggie had to give up the bin collection game after his wife had finally had enough of him coming home stinking of rubbish. With a heavy heart, he packed it in, and the entire East End came out to applaud his last bin collection.

Reggie became a bus conductor but was always unhappy in his new job. He missed the exciting cut and thrust of bin collecting. Fortunately, World War Two came along to help him out. In 1940 London was hit by the Blitz, and large parts of the East End found itself reduced to rubble thanks to the German Luftwaffe. With many locals away in the army, no one was available to do the bin collections and help with the clean-up. In his 70s, Reggie came out of retirement and was said to be just as quick as ever. The sight of a whistling Reggie emptying bins and clearing up rubbish lifted people's spirits and brought a smile back to their faces. In September 1940, Churchill visited the bombed-out areas of London and shook hands with the famous bin man.

After the war was won, Reggie took pride of place in a procession to celebrate VE Day and was awarded an MBE by the King, the first bin man to be given such an honour. He celebrated it by going to his local pub, hanging his medal over the bar, and getting drunk. When he died, the whole of the East End turned out to honour him, and his coffin was carried to the cemetery by a rear-loading bin lorry.

The Shortest War

Wars can last years and even decades. However, one conflict lasted only a few minutes. It was fought between two warring clans from Scotland: The Balfours and the Forresters.

In 1050 AD, after years of bickering over territory, taxes, and tartans, the two clans finally met each other in battle. Armed to the teeth with cudgels and pikes, they stood ready for action on opposing sides of a Scottish glen. The two chieftains, Baen of Clan Balfour and Rodric of Clan Forrester, rode forward to see if they could settle their differences.

The mood between the two men was tense until the ice was finally broken with a dirty joke. Faced with a bloody and costly battle, the two former friends buried the proverbial hatchet and agreed to one another's terms.

The time came to tell their armies to stand down and return to their villages peacefully. Unfortunately, Baen's brother-in-law was a bit of a half-wit. Rather than hoisting Clan Balfour's colours, as was the pre-agreed sign they'd signed a deal, he triumphantly waved his sword. Assuming they should attack immediately, the Balfour army roared their battle cry and charged down the hill. The opposing Forrester army unsheathed their weapons and attacked them in return.

Horrified at what they were witnessing, Baen and Rodric were trapped in the middle and vainly tried to halt the onrushing armies. The two clans met in the middle and began fighting as their leaders ran around shouting at their kinsmen to stop. In all the confusion, it took two minutes to halt the battle and reassert order.

When calm descended, a member of the Forrester clan had been sliced open and was dead. Baen and Rodric agreed that to keep the peace, the Balfours would volunteer a sacrificial lamb to even up the score. Still smarting over how the battle had kicked off, Baen offered up his brother-in-law. The unfortunate family member was dragged forward and run through with a pike.

Thus ended the two-minute war, and the matter was considered closed. The two clans headed home, although Baen had to do a bit of apologising to his sister.

The Biggest Pub Crawl

The Mongols were some of the most feared fighters in all of history. Their armies swept their way across Asia and the Russian steppe, killing and terrorising as they went. They emerged victorious in every battle they fought, thanks to their bravery and skill on a horse. By 1240, Kyiv had been sacked, and Europe appeared defenceless in front of the invaders. It seemed like the whole continent would fall victim to Mongol enslavement. But they were saved by an unlikely hero – booze.

Alcohol was not something the Mongols had sampled in their travels across Asia, but as soon as they reached Poland and Hungary, they discovered beer. At first, they were put off by the foul-smelling process that produced such a drink and caused people to spout nonsense and fall over. Then they tried it for themselves.

Just one sip and the Mongols were hooked. Although they had their own alcoholic drink from home called 'Airag'. It was made from fermented horse milk and tasted foul. By comparison, East European beer was loads better. The rest of the year descended into a massive booze cruise as the Mongols fought and drank across Europe, often going around in circles. Soon they were raiding taverns and alehouses, often spending days at a time drinking the place dry before struggling back onto their horses and zigzagging off in search of another. Of course, they never paid their bills, and the owner was lucky if he and his family were left alive to complain about it.

Booze was a bad influence on the Mongols. They would concoct macabre and brutal drinking games, which often resulted in someone losing a toe, a nose, or an even more valuable appendage. They were argumentative at the best of times, but when drunk, they were unstoppable and constant fights broke out between the different Mongol groups. One boozy brawl ended up costing the lives of 500 fighters, including a military warlord Sirqut Khan who was supposed to be leading the pillaging.

Slowly the invasion crawled to a stop. One battle had to be called off after half the Mongols stayed away, nursing hangovers and the other half were in such poor shape they were easily defeated. After six months of hard drinking, the Mongols were exhausted and enough was enough. Their bodies wrecked by booze and bad living, they clambered back on their horses and headed back across Asia. By the time they returned home, they had just about cleaned up, and many stayed teetotal for the rest of their days. Europe was just too much of a bad influence.

The Most Dangerous Coat Stand in History

Coat stands are considered pretty inoffensive objects. Yet one stand killed at least six people. And no one had any idea it was to blame.

The coat stand in question belonged to the Polish scientists Marie Curie and her French husband Pierre at the start of the 1900s. Based in Paris, the couple became famous pioneers in the field of radiation and were jointly awarded the Nobel Prize for Physics.

However, their success came at a cost. The damaging effects of radiation were not fully understood at the time, and their constant experiments with radioactive material emitted dangerous isotopes into the air. Without realising it, everything in their laboratory was poisoned with radiation, including a coat stand that the couple had bought when they first moved in. They even marked it with their initials at the bottom. The innocuous item stood in the corner of the laboratory, slowly absorbing radiation for over fifteen years until Pierre died in a road accident in 1906. After that, Marie decided to move premises and sell many of their belongings from the laboratory.

The radioactive coat stand found a new home with a history professor in his office. But after several years, he developed curious symptoms of fatigue and nausea, which mystified doctors. Encouraged to retire, the professor refused and continued working in his office as his symptoms worsened until he eventually died.

From there, his family donated the coat stand to a gentlemen's club in the heart of Paris, where the professor had been a member. Here it took pride of place in the entrance hall, holding the coats and hats of endless patrons as they passed through the club. One year later, the club started to develop a sinister reputation, as various members ended up collapsing and ended up in hospital. After spending time away from the club, they recovered, while three of its most regular members fell into a coma, sullying its reputation. No one dared enter its doors for fear of this mystery disease. The club went bankrupt, and its contents sold.

The coat stand was given to a local restaurant. There the same situation arose. Unexplained illnesses and two customer deaths led to health inspectors investigating the restaurant. Suspicion fell on the chef, who was driven mad with the idea that his cooking was somehow to blame, and he was committed to an asylum. The restaurant was boarded up, but only after the coat stand was handed to a second-hand furniture shop.

There it languished for several years under a mouldy rug until discovered by a painter who brought it back to his studio. From here, the artist might have gone the same way as previous victims; instead, his paintings saved him. After several months he noticed that oil paintings placed next to the coat stand would undergo discolouration over a period of time. Unsure of what was causing it, he put the coat stand in his attic and thought no more about it.

By now, nearly thirty years had passed since the stand had left the Curie's laboratory, and people were beginning to realise the harm that radiation caused. Following Marie's death from cancer in 1934, her scientific notebooks were found to be damaged by dangerously high radiation levels and were locked away. From photos taken of her laboratory, officials could identify the objects that had become contaminated. Her instruments, chair, desk, and even her blackboard was located and put into storage. Yet the Curie's coat stand was proving much harder to track down.

It took another twenty years for the coat stand to be located. By now, the painter had passed away, and his house was in the possession of his daughter. Hearing one day about the macabre legacy of the Curie's laboratory, she recalled the coat stand with magic powers that her father had told her about. Searching the dusty attic, she finally found what she was looking for and noticed a curious M & PC etched into the wood at the bottom. She'd discovered Marie and Pierre's coat stand.

Too dangerous to destroy, the stand was placed in a lead-lined storage box deep in the basement of the University of Paris, where it remains today along with Marie's other possessions. For safety reasons, no one is allowed to open the box and examine the coat stand, although if you're happy to wait, you might get a chance. Experts estimate that its radiation levels will be safe for humans in about 100,000 years. Presumably, by then, humans will have evolved away from the necessity of having coat stands.

Animals

The Parrot That Started a Revolution

Animals have played important roles in history, but none as pivotal as the parrot that kick-started a revolution.

Raul Hernandez was a military general who seized power in Honduras in 1880. He claimed he would govern for the people, yet after a decade under his rule, General Hernandez had only managed to enrich himself and his family. At the same time, the ordinary Hondurans were no better off.

While the citizens of Honduras starved in the streets, Hernandez built himself a marble presidential palace in the capital. Pride of place in the palace grounds was a giant zoo with over 20,000 wild animals. Hernandez took a particular liking to an exotic parrot and took the brightly coloured bird everywhere with him. He named him Hector after one of his defeated political opponents. The parrot spent so much time with the dictator that he started imitating his voice, much to the President's delight. The parrot was fond of repeating Hernandez's favourite command,

'Solo hazlo!', or 'Just get it done!' He would shriek this phrase at the President's underlings while Hernandez roared with laughter.

Outside the palace walls, the political situation was getting tense. In the summer of 1890, the capital saw rioting in the streets as people demanded a change in leadership. The President responded with a crackdown on the rioters, aggravating the situation. To deal with the stress, he drank rum and brandy throughout the night and gave strict orders for no one to enter his private rooms.

On the morning of the first of August, the largest crowd appeared outside the palace's main square, calling for the President to step down. Hundreds of troops were positioned in front of the unarmed protestors. The army chief frantically ran up to the President's bedroom to receive instructions on whether he should open fire. Standing outside the door he asked his leader whether he should go ahead. But unbeknownst to the chief, President Hernandez was still out cold in a drunken stupor. Instead, the parrot responded from his bedside table and told him, 'Just get it done!' The army chief asked him again, warning that this could make the situation a million times worse. All he heard was the President tell him even more loudly, 'Just get it done!'

And so, the regretful chief ordered the army to open fire, killing twelve people. The protestors were enraged by this reaction and rushed forward to overwhelm the soldiers and storm the palace. By now, the President was woken by the noise and demanded to know why the chief had opened fire. Realising what had happened, Hernandez became furious with the parrot and started chasing it around the palace, feathers and swearing flying through the air. He fired his revolver at the offending bird but kept missing until he smashed a window, and the parrot could escape. By this point, the protestors were ransacking the palace, and just as the parrot took flight, they stormed in and arrested the President. It seemed that Hector had had his final revenge. A revolution swept across the country and the President was tried for crimes against the people. He was hung in the same square that had seen the protestors fired on.

When the full story emerged, the parrot was tracked down to a nearby park. Some wanted it put on trial for its part in the killings, but luckily cooler heads prevailed. The parrot was set free and came to represent a historic emblem of the revolution. Streets were named in its honour, and jewellery portraying the bird was worn to commemorate the anniversary of when the Honduran people won their freedom.

The Cat Who Became a Ship's Captain

Cats have been respected and worshipped by many different cultures over the centuries. Only one cat was put in charge of a ship, though. It was all thanks to Federico Ramirez, the captain of a seventeenth century Spanish galleon that fought with the British navy up and down the coast of the Americas for colonial riches.

Captain Ramirez was obsessed with cats and believed them to be good luck. While running for his life through the streets of Santo Domingo, he came across a Manx cat that, in his view, led him to safety through the alleyways. He rewarded the plucky animal by bringing her aboard his ship, the Santa Martina, and named her Brisa, the Spanish for breeze.

Brisa proved to have excellent sea legs and kept the ship free from rats. As a bonus, the cat had a nose for dry land. When hiding from British forces in thick fog off Barbados, she stood at the boat's prow and pointed her nose in the correct direction to sail. The crew said that Brisa could smell rocks and dangerous shoals under the water, and they highly respected her. Everyone who served onboard got a tattoo of the special cat, and they even made her a leather jerkin to keep her warm.

Captain Ramirez treated the cat like his best mate, allowing her to dine with him on the finest foods and sleep in his bed. One time while moored off the coast of Costa Rica, the cat was lost ashore, and the ship spent an extra week at anchor while the frantic captain and his crew searched for their beloved cat. The boatswain eventually located Brisa lapping at a saucer of beer in a local tavern. As a rule, going AWOL would lead to a couple of days in the brig, but an exception was made for Brisa.

The ship was highly decorated in naval battles with the British. During these punch-ups, the cat was placed safely in the hold, although she often broke loose and could be seen running around the deck during the heaviest fighting. Most worryingly, the cat sometimes took to sleeping in the cannons, and the soldiers always checked to ensure they didn't blast the unfortunate feline out towards an enemy ship.

Rival captains offered the captain bags of doubloons to buy the cat, and he always refused, insisting that she was worth more than all the gold in the Americas. The cat was even presented to the Spanish King when the ship docked in Castellon following a successful voyage home.

In 1672 Captain Ramirez caught malaria and found himself near death. Soon enough, his condition worsened, and he said his final goodbyes to his cat and the crew. After he died, the ship's company read his will, which insisted that the cat be made captain. His men honoured the request and named Brisa as the new captain. The cat was listed as captain in the official records and was invited to drunken get-togethers with other Spanish captains. She was present at the signing of a peace treaty with the British in Florida.

The cat served as captain for another seven years until she died. In keeping with a captain's funeral, Brisa was buried at sea. It seemed that the cat had been lucky; only three months later, the ship ran aground and sank. As panicking men escaped in their row boats, and the ship's bow slipped beneath the waves, many swore blind that they heard the sound of a cat meowing.

The Cow That Voted in an Election

The British political system often stinks. And nothing smelled worse by the early 1800s than rotten boroughs. These were constituencies around the country that sent MPs to Parliament despite only having a handful of people living in them. They allowed corrupt landowners to bribe voters and buy entry into Parliament, while new cities like Manchester received no political representation.

In the 1826 general election, over a hundred MPs were elected by fewer than one hundred people voting in their constituency.

Campaigners and reformers demanded that this unfair system be swept away while the political establishment clung doggedly to the unfair influence they wielded. The political battle lines were drawn, and it all came to a head with the Old Mytleton affair.

Old Mytleton was a supposed Wiltshire village with no one living there. But in 1831, twenty-three registered voters successfully re-elected the Earl of Pickering to Parliament. The Earl had been the MP for Old

Mytleton for the last forty years and was notorious for never turning up to the House of Commons. The result seemed particularly fishy.

Closer inspection by reformers revealed that several of the voters had died years ago. As proof, their names were found on gravestones in the local church, while other voters had been made-up entirely.

The most glaring example of corruption was a voter named John Clacton, who turned out to be a cow. The records showed that 'John Clacton' had registered for the last three elections and voted for the Earl each time. The cow belonged to a local farmer who just happened to be the MPs' tenant.

The case of John Clacton became a political cause celebre. The reformers claimed this proved the absurdity of the rotten system. At the same time, supporters of Pickering were quick to push back, arguing that this was a very clever cow that knew a great deal about politics and was, therefore, perfectly entitled to vote. The farmer was summoned to substantiate these claims, insisting that the cow had always been interested in politics.

In the end, both sides agreed to an experiment to prove the political persuasion of the cow once and for all. A painting of the Prime Minister, Lord Liverpool, was posted to a fence at one end of the cow's field. For balance, a picture of his Whig opponent, the Marquess of Lansdowne, was placed on the other. Onlookers watched with bated breath to see which way the cow would go and which leader he would choose. Instead, John Clacton showed no interest in politics and headed straight for a delicious tuft of grass. He happily munched away, taking no notice of the Prime Minister.

By now, the arguments against reform were too ridiculous to maintain, and the government was forced to give way. The Great Reform Act removed many rotten boroughs, including Old Mytleton. The Earl of Pickering said goodbye to the House of Commons but was rewarded with a seat in the House of Lords, while John Clacton lived out his days in grassy comfort. He never voted in an election again.

The Horse That Swam the English Channel

In 1875 Matthew Webb became the first person to swim the English Channel. Yet it only took another decade for a horse to claim the same honour.

The successful horse in question was named Winchester and belonged to his Derbyshire owner William Phillis. With his horse business failing, Phillis stuck upon a novel idea that he believed would revive his fortunes and provide much-needed publicity. He announced that he would swim the English Channel on the back of his trusty steed. To practise for the endeavour, he swam a nearby lake over thirty times on Winchester's back and even developed a prototype buoyancy aid for his four-legged friend.

On the day of the undertaking, 12 May 1885, Phillis declared himself supremely confident of success. After a swig of brandy for the horse and its rider, William and Winchester set off from the Folkestone shore. Amazingly they went without a support boat, as William wanted his arrival to surprise the journalists waiting on the French side. He had signed a deal with the

London Times for exclusive photography rights to the tune of £100. Bystanders watched until the two disappeared from view.

It had taken Matthew Webb eighteen hours to make his crossing. However, twenty-four hours after setting off, neither horse nor rider had appeared, and it was assumed that both had perished. French fishermen were therefore astounded the next morning to discover an exhausted Winchester, still going a mile off the French coast, thirty-six hours after setting off.

Unfortunately, William Phillis was never seen again, a not particularly surprising outcome when you factor in that he couldn't even swim! Although suffering from hypothermia, Winchester fully recovered and lived out his days in happy retirement. The publicity his owner so desperately craved ended up going to his swimming companion, as Winchester basked in the fame of being the only horse to swim the channel. Tourists would pay a shilling to queue up and meet 'King Neptune's Steed' as he happily munched on hay.

The One and Only Space Pig

Everyone has heard of Laika, the Soviet space dog who, in 1957, became the first animal in space. Less well known is the pig that followed in Laika's four-legged footsteps.

Although Laika's mission was considered a success, the unfortunate canine died after six hours in orbit, and further animal missions were needed before human space flight could be attempted. Korolev, the mastermind behind the space program, felt that dogs weren't smart enough for some of the more advanced tasks required on the next mission. So, they decided to go with a pig after tests showed their high level of intelligence and reasonable behaviour.

Twenty pigs were selected, hand-picked from collective farms across the USSR after a 'talent show' call-out for clever pigs. Then a rigorous selection process whittled it down to two finalists. The pigs were trained to touch certain buttons with their snouts and received treats like grapes and apple slices as a reward. In the end, a Siberian black pig named Zvezda, meaning 'star', performed better under g-force conditions and won her place on the flight.

On 17 June 1959, Cosmonaut Zvezda took off from Kazakhstan and, within several hours, was orbiting Earth. Monitoring instruments showed that she was coping well with the conditions. This came with a problem. Zvezda was far too comfortable and refused to do any of her tasks. Mission control tried to cajole her through the intercom but to no avail. Instead, she had a nap. After receiving no further response, the mission eventually had to be cancelled. Thankfully it concluded with Zvezda's capsule parachuting safely back to Earth.

Zvezda's obstinacy proved the end of the animal program, and she retired from her role as a cosmonaut. Korolev adopted her, and she lived in his back garden. Zvezda was considered a good luck charm, and Yuri Gagarin patted her on the head before becoming the first human in space in 1961.

The Gardener Who Was killed by a Dinosaur

Humans and dinosaurs walked the Earth 65 million years apart and it seems unlikely you'd be harmed by one outside Jurassic Park. Yet in 1854, a dinosaur murdered an unlucky gardener, and it all was thanks to Queen Victoria's husband.

Prince Albert was an instrumental figure behind the Great Exhibition of 1851. Several years later, the Crystal Palace that housed the exhibition was moved to a permanent home in South London, which would go on to take its name. A series of dinosaur sculptures to be placed in the surrounding gardens were commissioned to accompany the opening. Palaeontology was hugely popular in Victorian England, and there was great public fascination to see these weird and wonderful creatures brought to life. The clay sculptures would be life-sized and built in a nearby workshop.

A year later, the opening of the new Crystal Palace was close at hand, but the sculptures were extremely heavy and proving difficult to move into position. Local labourers were ordered to help with the transfer when it fell behind. These included a gardener named George Clark, who had been working on the nearby flowerbeds. Finally, they had just one more dinosaur to move into place, the Iguanodon. This giant creation was more Komodo dragon than a dinosaur, with a lizard snout, a long body, and four clawed feet.

Tragically while moving the sculpture into place, one of the holding ropes snapped, and the Iguanodon fell to the ground, trapping George beneath its giant claws. Although eventually freed, the gardener died of his injuries soon after. His wife, Mary, was distraught and demanded compensation for her husband's death. Unfortunately, the company behind the Crystal Palace had no insurance, and the management refused to put their hand into their own pockets. Livid with this response, she took the company to court, and it seemed like she might win. Unluckily for her, the project's royal benefactor Prince Albert came to their rescue.

After a strong word from the Queen's husband, the authorities found a legal loophole to avoid paying the costs. The coroner ruled that George's death had technically been caused by a dinosaur rather than the project itself and that, ultimately, the Iguanodon was liable for any costs. The fact that it was a model dinosaur was conveniently left out of the ruling, so Mary's case collapsed.

The dinosaurs can still be seen in Crystal Palace, including the sculpture of the Iguanodon, which was hastily rebuilt. Although now considered widely inaccurate depictions, the models hide a darker secret – the time the royal family shafted a poor widow.

Nick Hall is a writer and comedian with a passion for the past.

Nick studied history at the University of Warwick before taking a master's degree in Russian Politics.

As a comedian Nick has written and performed for BBC2, BBC3 and BBC Radio 4, and has taken a number of shows to the Edinburgh Festival Fringe. These include the Cold War thriller 'Szgrabble' and 'Spencer', a character comedy telling the story of Spencer Percival, the only British Prime Minister ever to be assassinated. Nick has toured these shows around the country, and has performed at the Latitude Festival, Udderbelly Festival, Princes Trust, and Bloomsbury Theatre among others. Nick has also appeared on Sky News, The Times Red Box podcast, and written articles for the *Independent*.

Find him online:
Twitter: @nickhallsays
Website: www.thisisnickhall.com